L. F Liesching

A Brief Account of Ceylon

L. F Liesching

A Brief Account of Ceylon

ISBN/EAN: 9783337234454

Printed in Europe, USA, Canada, Australia, Japan

Cover: Foto ©Andreas Hilbeck / pixelio.de

More available books at **www.hansebooks.com**

A

BRIEF

ACCOUNT OF CEYLON.

BY

L. F. LIESCHING,

CEYLON CIVIL SERVICE.

And India's utmost isle, Taprobane.—MILTON.

Jaffna:

RIPLEY & STRONG,—PRINTERS.

1861.

TO

SIR CHARLES J. MACCARTHY,

GOVERNOR AND COMMANDER-IN-CHIEF

OF THE

Island of Ceylon and its Dependencies,

&c., &c., &c.

...rmission dedicated,

...uch respect, by

...Excellency's

...nt Servant,

THE WRITER.

CONTENTS.

GLOSSARY.

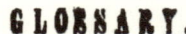

——

Da_ob_, a bell shaped monument enclosing a _____ Bu___.

Pansala, the monastic residence of Budhist _____

_____ **Budhist** t__

Sir Emerson Tennent has made the remark, that more works have been published on Ceylon, than on any other island in the world, England itself not excepted. Such being the case, the question may naturally be asked why it should have been thought necessary to add another to the number. To this we would reply that no book of a general character, has been written with a special view to the wants of those who ought to be chiefly interested in an account of the island,—namely, the sons of the soil. While the British Government has extended the benefits of European learning to its native subjects,—while the various missionary bodies have largely employed education as a means towards securing their great end,—and while the recipients of these benefits have learn to describe geographically, most countries in the world, and to give an historical account of several of them, they know little or nothing of that one in which they were born and bred.

There is in the history of Ceylon, much that is calculated to kindle the flame of patriotism, and to stir up its children to exertion. At a time when England was unknown to the greater part of Europe, and when the savages who inhabited it, painted on their bodies the figures of the sun, moon, and stars, Ceylon was the seat of civilization, the nursery of art, and the centre of commerce in the East. The ships of Rome, Arabia, Persia, India, and China floated in her waters,—the products of those various countries glittered in her marts. Her stupendous monuments, her agricultural works, the splendor of her courts, the wealth of her princes, the mildness of their sway, were the themes with which foreign ambassadors delighted the ears of their masters on their return. Should the reader, however, turn with longing eye to the days of old, and think of "the degeneracy of modern times," we would remind him that such structures as the dagobas of Anuradhapura and Pollonnarua, the pyramids of Egypt, the teocalis of Mexico, belong to a period of the world's history, far removed from this practical age :—that the construction of works for the irrigation of rice fields would not be the best mode of investing labor and capital in the present day ; and that the undertakings suitable to our times are our bridges, and our roads,—those arteries that convey between the centre of our system and its remotest extremities, the products that are as our life blood. We would bid him remember too, that no subjugated race now toils as the *Yakkos* of old, that their masters may enjoy themselves ; but that to all classes alike is acceded the liberty to do what they will, provided they interfere not with the equal rights of others.

There is little pretence to originality in these pages. The writer has freely made use of the labors of those who have gone before him and has freely acknowledged the sources of his information. Constant reference has been made to Sir Emerson Tennent's book, embodying, as it does, all that was known previously, as well as much that his extended research and unfailing activity have brought to light. The writer has not however blindly followed him, but has constantly, where the means existed for so doing, referred to those works to which Sir E. Tennent was himself indebted for his information ; and in some cases he has found it necessary to differ somewhat from the accomplished author of the book which has been so much and so justly admired and quoted of late.

In the humble confidence that this endeavor to place within the reach of every educated person in the island, a compendious account of Ceylon, will be favorably received, the writer sends forth this little book ; and it will not perhaps diminish any feeling of interest which may be excited by it to add, that it has been printed and bound by natives of Jaffna, who for some years past have had in their own hands, the press and binding establishments which formerly belonged to the American Mission, and who carry on their business, independently of foreign aid.

1. Sir E. Tennent's Ceylon.
2. Du____ Christianity in
   ____.
3. Cordiner.
4. Philalethes.
5. Percival.
6. Forbes.
7. Knox
8. Casie Chitty
9. Baldæus.
10. Ribiero.
11. Asiatic Society's Journal
12. Singhalese Tract Society's
    history

13. Ceylon Almanac.
14. Local Ordinances.
15. Sir Henry Ward's Minutes
16 Messrs. Bailey, Churchhill,
   and Adam's report.
17. Mullen's Hindu Philosophy.
18. Hardy's Eastern monach-
    ism
19. Mahawanse.
20. Rajawali.
21. Kyla'sa Ma'lai.
22. Gogerly's papers on Bud-
    hism.

BRIEF ACCOUNT OF CEYLON.

CHAPTER I.

Geographical position, Climate, Scenery, &c. of Ceylon.

CEYLON is an island, lying at the south-eastern extremity of the Peninsula of Hindustan, from which it is separated by Palk's Straits and the Gulf of Manaar.

A string of shoals called "Adam's Bridge," extending from the Island of Manaar on the Ceylon side, to the Island of Ramesuram on the Indian side, prevents the passage of vessels; and it is only by incessant dredging that a narrow channel between Paumben and the mainland of India is kept open for ships of light draught.

The most northerly point of Ceylon is Pt. Palmyra, in latitude 9°, 51'; and the most southerly is Dondera Head, in latitude 5°, 55', north of the equator. Its most easterly point is Sangemankande, in longitude 81°, 54', 55', and its most westerly is Colombo, in longitude 79°, 41', 40', east of Greenwich. Its extreme length is 271½ miles, and its greatest breadth, 137½ miles. Its area, including the islands on its north-western coast, is 25,742 square miles.

Among the many names by which Ceylon has been known, are Taprobane, Zerendib, and Zielan. It is called by the Singhalese, Singhale Dwipe, and Lanka; and by the Tamuls, Elankai.

The scenery, climate, and vegetation of Ceylon, vary considerably. In the north, the country is flat, the air dry, the soil light, and spontaneous vegetation comparatively scanty. Along the south-western and southern sea boards, the view is diversified, the air humid, and the foliage dense. On the east coast, about Trincomalie, hill and valley, wood and water, are mingled in a manner picturesque beyond description. As we advance farther into the interior, the undulations of the coast swell into mountains of considerable size. Here the traveller enters the regions of forests and running water; mist and rain alternate with bursts of glowing sunshine; the air is keen and bracing; the scenery bold and striking.

The highest mountains in Ceylon are:

Pethuru Tallegalle, in height	-	8,280	Eng. feet.
Kirigal Potte	"	-	7,810	"
Tottapelle	"	-	7,720	"
Adam's Peak	"	-	7,420	"
Namone Koole	"	-	6,740	"

Almost the whole of the Central province however, is a succession of ranges of hills, covering in all, an area of 4,212 square miles.

Where there are mountains, we naturally expect to find rivers. Of these, the three largest are:

The Mahawelliganga	134	miles in length.
The Kalaniganga	84	"
The Kaluganga	72	"

These three rivers take their rise near Adam's Peak in the Saffragam district. The Mahawelliganga passes by Kandy, meanders through the jungles of Bintenne, and empties itself into the sea near Trincomalie. The Kalaniganga discharges itself at Mutwal, a few miles north of Colombo. It is navigable for boats to the foot of the mountains at Ambegamoa. The Kaluganga flows by Cultura, and is navigable for boats to Ratnapoora.

Next to these three, are the following :

Name of river.	Length.	Place where it enters the sea.
The Dideroo Oya	70 miles	Near Chilaw.
The Welleway	69 "	Near Hambantotte.
The Maha Oya	68 "	Near Negombo.
The Kirinde	62 "	Near Mahagam.
The Gindura	59 "	Near Galle.
The Nievalle	42 "	Near Matura.
The Bintereganga	. . .	Near Bentotte.

All these rivers take their rise amongst the mountains of the interior; but there are others, which as Sir Emerson Tennent says, belong to the plains of the northern and south-eastern portions of the Island, and are, not unfrequently shaded, of formidable size. Of these, the principal are, the Modregam and the Aruvy, which flow into the Gulf of Manaar ; the Kalu Oya and the Kandalady, which terminate in the Bay of Calpentyn ; the Kattregam, and the Kamboakam opposite the little Bass rocks ; and the Navaloor, the Patipal Aar, the Chadawak, and Arookgam, south of Batticaloa.

At intervals along the seaboard of the island, the traveller meets with lakes which are generally speaking

formed by the waters from the interior spreading themselves over the low ground near the sea, from which a
bar of sand usually separates them. Over this, the
fresh waters at certain periods force their way, and flow
into the ocean : at other times the sea has the mastery,
washes over the bar, and renders the lake more or
less salt. Such was probably at one time, the case with
the Colombo lake ; but means having been adopted
to prevent the entrance of the sea, it is now always
fresh. Between Colombo and Galle several sheets of
water are to be met with, of the nature described. What
is commonly called the Jaffna lake, is however of a different character. It is properly speaking, a lagoon or
shallow inlet of the sea, subject to the influences of the
tides, and entirely independent of any addition to its vol-
ume from rivers, of which indeed there are none in the
Peninsula.

The Island of Ceylon has been artificially divided into six provinces ;—the Western, the North-western, the
Northern, the Eastern, the Southern, and the Central.

The principal places in each will be described in the
following pages.

Colombo, the capital of the island, is situated in the
Western Province, on the sea coast, a little below the 7th
degree of north latitude. It enjoys the benefit of a delightful sea-breeze, during the prevalence of the south-
western monsoon. The temperature varies from 76° to
$86\frac{1}{2}$° Faht., but the winds considerably mitigate the
heat. Frequent showers maintain a constant verdure,
except during the months of February, March and
April, when those Europeans who can do so, betake
themselves to the mountain regions.

The Colombo lake forms an agreeable feature in the scenery of the place; its banks are dotted with the residences of European gentlemen, who, confined for the greater part of the day to their close offices within the Fort, escape, after business hours, to their homes, which are either, as already said, on the lake, in the cinnamon gardens which adjoin it, or on the sea-shore.

The Eurasians principally occupy the Pettah, which is regularly laid out after the manner of Dutch towns, in streets parallel, or at right angles to each other. A mixed population inhabits the rest of the town.

The Governor resides within the Fort; which also contains the barracks of the European troops, most of the public and mercantile offices, the Banks, a Library, and a Chamber of Commerce; an Episcopal, a Presbyterian, and a Wesleyan place of worship. The Malay troops are quartered about a mile off, at a place called Slave island.

Galle, the chief town of the Southern Province, is about 72 miles south of Colombo. The fort is built on a strip of land, projecting into the sea.

The situation of Galle marks it at once as the natural halting station for the steamers which ply between Suez, Bombay, Calcutta, China, and Australia. It is consequently a place of much resort. The natives in the neighborhood are expert in the manufacture of ebony work boxes inlaid with ivory and the various valuable woods for which the Island is celebrated, as well as of tortoise shell combs, bracelets, &c. &c., which realize handsome prices.

The scenery about Galle is picturesque, and the climate humid. A disease of a very distressing nature prevails there, called elephantiasis. The main symptom is the swelling of one or both legs to an enormous size. The natives attribute it, rightly or wrongly, to the quality of the water.

The investigations of Sir Emerson Tennent have led him to believe that Galle was the Tarshish of Scripture, whence the ships of Solomon carried ivory, apes, and peacocks. The reasons assigned if not conclusive, are in favor of the supposition.

Trincomalie, the capital of the Eastern Province, is situated on the east coast. Its harbor is one of the finest in the world. It is land locked; and so deep is the water even close to the shore, that vessels of the largest tonnage may lie close alongside the naval yard, which has there been constructed for the use of Her Majesty's ships in the Indian seas. Its name is thought by some to be a corruption of Terukonatha malai or the mountain of the sacred Konather, in whose honor a temple, celebrated throughout India, once stood within the limits of what is now called Fort Frederick; but its name is in reality derived from Tirikona malai, or the three coned mountain. Fort Frederick, which commands the Back and Dutch bays, is protected on the side facing the open sea, by a projecting cliff, on which a flag staff and light house are erected. From the verge of this eminence, the eye looks down a declivity of several hundred feet, sheer into the boiling surf below. There is a monument on its summit, to the memory of a Dutch girl called Francina van Reede; and tradition says, that the hapless damsel threw herself over this fearful precipice, in sight of her faithless lover, as he sailed from the harbor at her feet, on his way to other lands.

The coast about Trincomalie is indented by numerous bays. The Inner harbor, commanded by Fort Ostenberg, is studded with islands, one of which is called Sober Island, where there is a pleasantly situated bungalow, kept up by the naval officers on the station.

The geological features of Trincomalie are remarkable. The jungle in its neighborhood is dense, and extends to the very water's edge ; and wild animals including elephants and cheetas, are to be met with close to the town. The scenery is beautiful ; but the heat for a great part of the year, is intense ; for the town is shut in by hills, and the soil consists of quartz, each particle of which acts as a minute mirror, in reflecting the rays of the sun. During the prevalence of the north-east monsoon, which, on this coast is the sea breeze, as the south west is on the opposite side of the island, the climate is delightful ; and the loveliness of the country and the facilities for water excursions, offer inducements for pleasure parties such as no other part of the low country affords.

About seven miles from Fort Frederick at a place called Kannia, are six hot springs which though varying in temperature from 98° to 160° Faht., are evidently connected with each other.

The town of Jaffna, the principal station in the Northern Province, is 221 miles north of Colombo, on the southern side of the peninsula of the same name, and on the shore of the lagoon called the Jaffna lake. Owing to the shallowness of the water, vessels usually unload their cargoes at the other ports in the district. The fort is a neat and compact structure, built by the Dutch after a plan of Vauban. The outer facings are constructed of square blocks of coral, a substance which is abundant in the peninsula. It admits of being cut into any required shape, with the saw and adze, and hardens on exposure to the air.

The peninsula of Jaffna is intersected by excellent roads, and the facilities for making them are greater than in any other part of the Island, on account of the comparative cheapness of labor, the abundance of material, and the absence of engineering difficulties. We may observe parenthetically here, that the excellence of the roads throughout the Island is always a subject of remark with strangers, and is highly creditable to the Government, and the department of public works.

The scenery about Jaffna differs considerably from that of the rest of the Island. The diversity of hill and dale is entirely wanting; rivers and streams are unknown. It has however beauties of its own. No where else in Ceylon has agriculture been carried to such perfection. Viewed through a crystal atmosphere, neighboring objects stand out in relief with a clearness of outline remarkable even in the tropics. The islands and headlands seen across the smooth lagoon, at times seem to hang in air, so imperceptibly do sky and water meet; the landscape appears rather a mirage than a reality, and the soft sun-sets, the still air, and the silent avocations of the agriculturist, suggest the idea of repose and calm.

We must content ourselves with a very brief account of the smaller towns and ports along the sea coast, before proceeding to the interior.

Going southward from Colombo, we arrive first at

Pantura, a thriving and busy little place about 15 miles from the capital. It has a police court and a custom house.

Caltura comes next, a pleasant and salubrious locali- ty, 26 miles from Colombo, on the banks of the Kalu- ganga. It is a district judge's station, and has also a Custom house. The dilapidated fort is used as a jail.

Barbaryn is a port of entry, between Caltura and Bentotte; the latter, famed for its oysters, is 38 miles from Colombo on the south bank of the Bentere river, which separates the Western from the Southern Pro- vince.

Balipitye Modera, between Bentotte and Galle, is a sea port, and magistrate's station.

Dodandowe is a small port, eight miles north of Galle.

Proceeding eastward from Galle, we come to Belli- gam, a customs station, 16½ miles from Galle; and thence we proceed to Matura, 11 miles further, the re- sident station of an assistant agent. The spirit of liti- gation must be strongly developed about Matura, for it is the only place in the Island where there are two dis- trict judges.

Gandura is a port between Matura and Tangalle.

Tangalle is about 23 miles east of Matura, and is a district judge's station.

Hambantotte, the last place of note in the Southern Province, lies on the shores of a large bay, and is 79 miles east of Galle. An assistant agent resides here, as well as a commandant in charge of a detach- ment of the Ceylon Rifles. The extensive salt pans in its neighborhood supply a great part of the island with that necessary of life.

Batticaloa is the first town in the Eastern Province, which the traveller reaches after leaving Hambantotte; the distance between them is upwards of 154 miles. The town is built on an island in the lake, which island is about three and a half miles in circumference, and is called Puliantivu. The fort has been converted into a residence for the assistant government agent. A district judge is stationed there. The distance from Trincomalie is upwards of 106 miles by land.

Mullitivu, is a small station between Trincomalie, and Point Pedro. It belongs to the Northern Province, and one officer discharges the united duties of assistant agent, magistrate, and collector of customs.

Point Pedro is 21 miles from Jaffna, at the extreme north of the Island. It is a thriving place of trade, and has a police court and a custom house : but the town of Velvattetorre, 4½ miles west of it, threatens to outstrip it in commerce. The port of Kangeysentorre lies between this place and Kayts, which is a sea port, and magistrate's station.

Manaar, built on an island of the same name, is separated from the mainland by a shallow channel, between two and three miles broad. It lies about 167 miles north of Colombo. An assistant to the government agent of the Northern Province is stationed there, as well as a sub-collector of customs. It has a small fort.

Leaving the Northern Province, the first town in the North-western is that of Calpentyn, built on the peninsula which forms the western boundary of the gulf of Calpentyn. It is a Magistrate's and a customs' officer's station and has a small fort.

Putlam, formerly the head quarters of the government agent for the North-western Province, and now an assistant agency, is about 85 miles north of Colombo. There are extensive salt pans in its vicinity.

Chilaw is 53 miles north of Colombo, and is a district judge's station.

Negombo is about 23 miles north of Colombo, on the shores of an extensive lake. It is a thriving town, inhabited by a population which speaks both Singhalese and Tamil; but more commonly the latter. The fort has been converted into a court house for the resident district judge. The Roman Catholics are in great force, and have many churches here. The district of Negombo, belongs to the Western Province.

We now proceed to the inland towns. Kandy, the capital of the Central Province, lies 72 miles distant from Colombo in ·a north-easterly direction, in a basin amidst the mountains. It is called by the Singhalese, Maha Newera, or the great city. It probably derives the name "Kandy" by which it is known amongst Europeans, from the Singhalese word " *Kande*," a mountain; and the foreigners applied to the town, the word intended only to denote its locality.

The scenery about Kandy is very beautiful, and an artificial lake constructed by a Singhalese king, forms a pleasing feature in the view from the neighboring hills. The " Pavilion," as ·the official residence of the Governor is called, is a handsome edifice surrounded by a tasteful garden. It is·generally occupied during the hot months of the year. Well constructed churches, barracks, public buildings, and European dwelling houses, are intermingled with Budhist temples, and native houses;

the slopes of the surrounding hills are dotted with bungalows, and coffee estates, and the whole scene is calculated to produce a striking effect on the mind of a
stranger.

The climate of Kandy is very changeable. The morn-
ings and evenings are cool and even cold, and the dews
very heavy, while the days are often intensely warm.
Frequently a sudden shower accompanied by a chill
breeze, soaks to the skin in a few seconds, those who
have just before been sweltering beneath a blazing sun.
Situated moreover in a hollow, the vapors of evening
accumulate and hang over the town, whilst the hills
about it are clear.   The consequence is, that fever and
dysentery are at certain seasons prevalent, and the climate
though more bracing, is more insidious than that of the
sea coast.   As most of the towns in the interior are
built in valleys amidst tracts of paddy field, the same
remark applies equally to them.   The coffee estates
however, which are almost invariably situated on the
sides of the hills, are far more healthy, and many of
them can boast of a climate equal to any in the world.

Kandy is the heart of the coffee districts, and is consequently a place of much resort and activity.

Gampola is a thriving little place within 18 miles of
Kandy on the Newera Ellia road; a handsome new
bridge has recently been erected over the Mahavelli
Ganga, which passes the town.

Newera Ellia, is a sanitarium 6,202 feet above the
level of the sea, at the foot of the mountain called Pethuru Tallegalle, the highest in the Island.   The roads
and the residences of the Europeans, are built on their
surrounded by thickly wooded hills.   The air is always

keen at this elevation, and ice and frost are formed during the night, at certain seasons of the year. Potatoes, cauli-flowers, pease, strawberries, and various other European vegetables and fruits are cultivated with success, and fires are enjoyable for the greater part of the year. A scanty native population is located there, consisting chiefly of bazaar keepers; but the cold and wet prevent more from coming; some English settlers have adopted the place as their home, and cultivate the soil with profit and success. An attempt was made by two gentlemen, the Messrs. Baker, to carry on farming on a large scale; but it proved a failure. European invalid troops are quartered there, and the wealthier families from the low country spend the hot months in this invigorating but expensive station. An assistant to the government agent of the Central Province, and a commandant, reside there. Its distance from Colombo is 111, and from Kandy, 47 miles. The thermometer ranges from 36° to 62°, and never rises above 70° in the shade.

Badulla, once the capital of the principality of Uva, is 84½ miles south-east of Kandy, and about 37 miles from Newera Ellia. It lies at the foot of the mountain called Namene Koole, amidst an extensive tract of paddy land. The view on approaching it is very beautiful, and indeed there are scenes in the district of Uva, unsurpassed by any in the Island. The natural features on the Kandy side of the Newera Ellia range are often grand and awe inspiring; but on the Badulla side, the sublime and the picturesque are united. Badulla is the head quarters of an assistant agent, a district judge and a commandant; the coffee estates in its vicinity promise to render it ere long, a place of some importance.

Retracing our steps to Kandy, and proceeding in a northerly direction, we first reach Matele, a thriving town 16 miles from the Central capital, in the midst of a flourishing coffee district; an assistant agent resides there.

Passing the police court station of Dambool, 45 miles from Kandy, the next place of note which the traveller reaches is Anuradhapura, of which more will be said hereafter. At present this once famous city is the residence of a single civil servant, who unites in himself the duties of the revenual and judicial departments. It is 90 miles from Kandy, and eight miles west of the central road to Jaffna. Though a Singhalese District, it is revenually attached to the Northern Province.

Kurnegalle lies at the foot of an immense mass of rock, 26 miles to the north-east of Kandy. It is the place of residence of the government agent for the North-Western Province; a district judge, and a military officer with a small party of riflemen are stationed here

Ratnapura, or the city of gems, is situated on the banks of the Kalaniganga, 56 miles from Colombo, in a south-easterly direction, in the vicinity of Adam's Peak. It is celebrated for the gems found in its neighborhood. It forms part of the Western Province, and an assistant agent resides there.

Avishavelle, a police magistrate's station, is 30 miles from Colombo, on the road to Ratnapura.

Kaigalle is an assistant agency attached to the Western Province, 49 miles from Colombo, on the main road to Kandy.

Chavagacherry and Mallagam, are two magistrates' stations in the Northern Province; the first about 11 miles east, and the other about 8 miles north-west of the town of Jaffna. With them, ends our sketch of the inland towns and stations.

Among the designations of the Queen's representative, we meet with the words, " Governor and Commander-in-Chief of the Island of Ceylon *and its dependencies.*" This latter term applies to Manaar, and the islands north of Adam's bridge, adjacent to Ceylon. They are Mand-iti'vu, Ve'lene, Karati'vu, Eluveiti'vu, Analei'ti'vu, Ny-nati'vu, Pungerti'vu, Iranati'vu, and Nedunti'vu or Delft. Besides these, there are several islets, too insignificant to mention particularly.

CHAPTER II.

The Inhabitants and Residents of Ceylon.

INHABITANTS.

The Inhabitants of Ceylon belong to the following races.
1. The Veddahs, 2. The Singhalese, 3. The Tamils,
4. The Moormen, 5. The Eurasians.

The Veddahs are placed first, because there is good
reason to believe they are the aborigines. They inhabit
that part of the island called Bintenne, lying between
Batticaloa and the mountain region. They live by the
chase, and dislike a settled life. Their weapons are the
bow and arrow; and with these they destroy deer,
monkeys, buffaloes, and even elephants. They are tol-
erably expert marksmen within sixty yards, but an
English archer with his superior implements would easily
surpass them. Their stature is low, and their appearance squalid. They preserve their game in wild honey,
with which the forests abound. The arts of woodcraft
are thoroughly understood by them. The rock Veddahs
shun unnecessary intercourse with strangers. Efforts
have been made to reclaim some of them in the neighborhood of Batticaloa, with partial success; the love of
a nomadic life is however too strong to permit them to
settle down to agriculture. They have no religion save
a fear of devils. They are decreasing in number, and
will eventually die out. The attempts made to reclaim
the village, as well as the coast Veddahs, have been
more successful; the latter live by fishing, and felling
timber.

The Singhalese may be subdivided into three classes.

the maritime or low country Singhalese ; the Kandians ; and the Rodias or outcastes.

The low country Singhalese occupy the sea coast of
the Western and Southern Provinces. They are a handsome and well made race, and their appearance and
character are gentle, rather than bold or hardy. Nature
has been bountiful to them, and their wants are readily
supplied. This very bounty however has been unfavorable to the development of active habits and enterprise.
The cultivation of the soil is the favorite pursuit of the
Singhalese, and in landed property it is that they best
love to invest their money. They are by no means defi-
cient in quickness or talent, and when educated, make
good scholars. The turn of their minds is metaphysical
and speculative. They have naturally a great aptitude
for figures, and readily acquire a knowledge of mathematics. Their national religion is Budhism ; though
there are many converts to Christianity among them.
The ordinary dress of the men is a white or colored
cloth called a comboy, folded round the lower part of the
body, and depending below the knee more or less, according to the caste of the wearer. The hair is allowed
to grow, and is tied in a knot at the back of the head,
where it is secured by a large tortoise shell comb similar
to that worn by European ladies some thirty years ago ;
a small semi-circular comb in front of the large one, com-
pletes their head dress. The better orders assume the
European coat, either of modern cut, or of the old Dutch
pattern, with gold buttons and gold worked button holes ;
and many of them have adopted the European costume,
in toto ; but generally wear in addition, the comb and the
comboy. This union of costumes is incongruous in the

eyes of foreigners; but the Singhalese are reluctant to renounce these distinctive marks of their race.

The highest rank amongst them is that of Modeliar. It is either borne ex-officio, or is conferred by the Governor as an honorary distinction. On state occasions the Modeliars attend Government house in full costume; when they wear handsomely ornamented curved dirks, suspended from the shoulder by richly worked gold belts. Some of them wear round their necks golden medals of considerable size, bearing an inscription commemorative of services rendered to Government by the wearers or their ancestors, on account of which the medal was presented to them.

Many of the Singhalese have Portuguese names; such as De Zylva, De Lewera, De Saram, Gomez, Fonseka, Dins, &c. These names were assumed by their ancestors, at their baptism, with the sanction of their Portuguese god-fathers. The manners of the Singhalese are gentlemanly and polished in the extreme, and many of them are highly informed, and agreeable in conversation. The houses and tables of the higher classes, are furnished in English style, and on festive occasions are decorated most tastefully by means of garlands, and the young leaves of the cocoanut, and by transplanting plantain and other trees, which retain their verdure sufficiently long to produce a very beautiful effect, when lighted by lamps symmetrically arranged among them.

The Budhist priests invariably wear a yellow robe, and have their heads closely shorn, in whatever part of the Island they may be. The Singhalese women generally wear a short jacket and a comboy and

their long and glossy hair with gold or silver pins, and
sometimes a small prettily worked comb. The wealthier wear white slippers with high heels, and a profu-
sion of jewelry, when they go abroad. No covering
for the head is used by them.

The Kandians are as a body, hardier and more robust
than their brethren of the low country, though of the
same race. Breathing the bracing air of the hills which
they are constantly ascending and descending, their
limbs are wiry and their habits active. Their ordinary dress is a cloth round the loins. They never wear
the comb, and their beards are allowed to grow.
Their chiefs envelope themselves in an immense quantity of muslin, wound again and again around the waist
and allowed to fall in folds to the ankle. When in full
dress, they wear a jacket with wide giggot sleeves, a ruff,
and a peculiarly shaped hat, somewhat resembling two
saucers laid one on the other, with the rims meeting,
made either of white or black cloth, and ornamented
with silver or gold ornaments. The dress of the women
consists of a cloth, which they fold gracefully about
them; their hair is tied in a knot hanging down rather
low at the back of the head, and they are fond of jewelry.

The homesteads of the Kandians are often substantial
buildings, forming a quadrangle which faces inwards,
whitewashed and thatched with straw, sheltered by um-
brageous trees in a nook of the valley, and surrounded
by tracts of rice land, terraced up the neighbouring
hills, and irrigated by streams which flow into them;
and their herds of small black cattle and buffaloes
graze on the slopes. In some districts, especially in
Oodilla, which is comparatively a dry one, water is led

in channels for miles along the sides of the hills, to irri-gate the fields which are remote from streams.

The spirit of independence is strongly developed in the Kandians, and their attachment to their hereditary lands is extraordinary. Nothing will induce a Kandian to sell his patrimony; and he will spend pounds willing-ly in law-suits, to secure a slip worth a few pence. This characteristic is not to be lost sight of, in forming an opinion of the people. It is one strongly developed in most Asiatics, but peculiarly so in the Kandians. They are averse to servile employment, and though they might secure high wages on the European coffee estates, they prefer earning a subsistence by cultivating their own patches of land. The only occupation they will undertake is felling forest, at which they are very ex-pert. The coffee estates are consequently worked by coolies from the Malabar coast. They have very little practical acquaintance with the arts and manufactures; enough of carpentry and blacksmith's work is understood among them, to enable their workmen to mend a plough or prepare the timber for a house; but they readily buy European articles, and money is by no means scarce with many of them. They are fond of burying what substance they possess under the earth in chatties. The spot is often known only to the head of the house, and there are instances where he has come to an untimely end, and the secret has died with him.

Education has not made the same progress among the Kandians that it has in the maritime districts. The villagers are consequently very superstitious and very credulous. Polygamy and polyandry were till lately toler-ated; but to the credit of the chiefs and influential people be it said that they have themselves petitioned the Government to pass a law depriving this practice of legal recognition for the future. A state of feudal tenure still prevails, resembling in some respects that which existed in Europe of old. There are chiefs who own tracts of country, and whole villages, the inhabitants of which are bound to do certain services for their tenures. In the neighborhood of Kandy and in the town itself, the influences of European civilization extend to the natives, and there are Kandian gentlemen whose manners and habits are entirely English.

The Rodias are included amongst the Singhalese, for want of better information about them. Knox, who was a captive among the Kandians for nearly twenty years, says that they were persons whose duty it was to supply the king with game; and that on one occasion they produced human flesh, which His Majesty enjoyed so much that he directed them to procure more of what he supposed was part of a wild animal. The deception became known however to the royal barber, who acquainted the king with it. The rage of the king may be imagined; and, as the direst punishment he could inflict on the offenders, he decreed that henceforth they, as well as all their tribe, should be outcastes from other society; that they should not be allowed to pursue any calling, but beg their bread from door to door, and be shunned by others. This order of things being once established, it became no unusual practice for the king to punish noble men and women who incurred his displeasure, by condemning them to join the Rodias with their whole families, a sentence worse than death. This fact may ac-

count for the beauty of form peculiar to this class, in
spite of the abject demeanor which their degraded position superinduces. It is thought by some that they were
originally a separate race, in fact, the aborigines. Knox
who must no doubt have had many opportunities of
learning about them, gives in his truthful and quaint
way, the traditions common in his time. He says they
were originally " Dodda Veddahs, which signifies hun-
ters." Now Dodda is probably Knox's mode of pronounc-
ing the Singhalese name for game : they were called
" Game *Veddahs*." If then a branch of the Veddah
tribe, most probably they were the descendants of
the aborigines ; and whereas the other Veddahs, occu-
pying the feverish jungles of Bintenne, and carrying on
a hard struggle with privation and hunger, have become
more squalid in appearance, these being recruited by
noble families, and living in a healthier part of the Island,
have improved rather than deteriorated in form. The
Rodias live in villages of their own, and obtain their
subsistence by begging ; their importunity and the aver-
sion with which they are regarded being in their favor ;
for people are glad to purchase their departure by a
gratuity. They have the credit moreover of being expert thieves, and on that account too, the fact of a Rodia
locating himself near a Singhalese village, which under
the present Government there is nothing to prevent his
doing, occasions considerable excitement and indignation.
Having formerly been debarred from tilling the soil, they
have learnt to make articles of handicraft, such as grass
ropes, baskets, and mats. They also make strong hide
ropes for securing cattle and wild elephants. This was
a service they were obliged to render the Kandian kings ;

consequently they claimed the carcases of all the cattle that died; and it is said that this is their favorite food, especially when in a *high* condition. From the fibre of a species of aloe they also manufactured whips which were carried before the great in processions, and cracked with a noise like the report of a pistol. The women are expert at such feats as spinning brass plates on one finger, tossing balls in the air and catching them, &c. At the great festivals in Badulla, when thousands of persons both men and women, are assembled, the Rodias who come as spectators can always be distinguished at a glance. The Singhalese women on these occasions go hand in hand, some four or five being thus strung together; and the reason assigned is that they are afraid of being kidnapped by the Rodias. Their habits of life are said to be unnatural and immoral. In former days the women were only allowed to cover the lower part of the person, but this prohibition no longer exists, and they generally wear a colored silk handkerchief tied round the neck and waist. Their figures are erect as arrows. One can hardly view a race so fine in a physical point of view,—so degraded in a moral aspect, without pity, and a desire to see them raised. It will be long before the Kandians learn to regard them with any other than their present feelings. The men might find employment on the public roads, but they are averse to labor. There are words in use among them not spoken by the Singhalese generally. Mr. Simon Casie-chitty in an interesting article on these people in the Asiatic Society's Journal, gives upwards of 100 words peculiar to them. It would be interesting to enquire whether any of these words are also in use among the Veddahs.

The Tamils occupy all the Northern Province except the district of Newerekalawa, and all the Eastern, with the exception of the Veddah country and the southern part of the Batticaloe district. They originally came over from the eastern part of India. They retain the Tamil language and the Hindu religion. They differ from the Singhalese in appearance, manners, and dress, and though they assimilate to the Tamils of India, a practised eye can at once detect a difference. They do not as a rule cultivate the beard and moustache, and their frames are more robust and thickset than their lithe and jaunty looking cousins over the sea. The seamen are a remarkably well made class, with broad chests, fearless bearing, and muscular limbs. A cloth round the waist and a turban, are the ordinary dress of the poorer classes, and the latter is often dispensed with. The hair is worn long, and fastened in a knot, which bachelor dandies love to adjust over one ear. An oleander flower or rose stuck behind the ear is also a mark of attention to appearance. The school boys often encircle the head with the strip of ola on which their lesson is written. The highest official office is that of Maniagar, and the second that of Odiar. These officers are for the most part distinguished by a turban ironed smooth instead of being folded loosely, and arranged in a peculiar form somewhat like a cross. It is said that this practice was introduced by the Portuguese as a mark of the conversion of the wearers to Christianity. If so, the dress has survived the religion. The richer classes are accustomed to wear several sets of massive gold ear-rings, and occasionally an amulet curiously wrought, on the arm ; gold contrasts well with the dark Asiatic skin. They sometimes rub scented sandal wood on their chests; ashes applied to the forehead, chest and arms, as well as the caste mark on the forehead, are essentially marks of heathenism ; and to say of one who was a convert to Christianity that he has " rubbed ashes," is equivalent to saying he has relapsed.

The Brahmins or priestly caste, shave the head, with the exception of a long tuft on the crown, and invariably wear a cotton string across the shoulder in a particular and distinctive manner. The tuft has however been cultivated of late by many not of the Brahmin caste. The color of the Brahmins is lighter than that of the people generally. They do not in Ceylon as in India, engage in secular employment as a general rule.

The educated classes and those employed in Government offices, wear a neat and tasteful dress, consisting of a curiously folded turban, a short bodied and full skirted white coat and white trousers, with a silk handkerchief or a scarf round their necks. The women of the higher orders envelope themselves in a muslin or silk cloth, gracefully arranged over the head and shoulders. Their hair is secured by gold or silver pins, their arms and ankles are encircled by bangles, their fingers and toes by rings and their necks by necklaces of various kinds. Their ears are adorned with ear-rings or ear-pins, and the nose is often perforated to admit of a jewelled pendant. The poorer women wear a piece of white cloth wound round them, thrown over the shoulder and kept in its place by a heavy key dangling behind. The married women wear a necklace called a thaly which corresponds with

the English wedding ring and is even more sacredly
guarded. The Tamils are industrious and enterprising,
and their seaports carry on a brisk trade with India.
Considerable progress has been made in education, and
their minds are capable of receiving any kind of knowledge with readiness. The cultivators pay much attention
to their fields and gardens. Constant irrigation and man-
uring are essential, and they possess a very fair amount of
practical acquaintance with agriculture and horticulture.
In a country where running water is unknown, the people
are dependent on wells; and their mode of irrigation is
simple and curious. A long wooden "sweep" is suspended over the well, with a rope and basket attached
to one end, and this basket is lowered by a man who
alternately advances and recedes, standing on the
" sweep." Another man below, empties the water into
a channel which is carried among the plants in the
garden. The "sweep" is so adjusted that one end is
heavier than the other, and when the basket is full of
water the sweep is nearly balanced. In the remoter parts
of the Jaffna district, the supply of water for the year is
collected in tanks during the rainy season.

The Eurasians or Burghers are either descended from
pure Dutch parents who made the island their home, or
are the offspring of European and native alliances. The
term " Burgher" signifies in Dutch a citizen or one entitled to the freedom of the borough. At present it is applied generally to all having any European blood, who were
born in the island of colonial parents. There is naturally a very great diversity in a class falling under so
general a designation, and its members range from the
retired district judge or sitting magistrate, who still re-

tains the recollection of his former position and that of his ancestors, and who has not forgotten their language, to the humble artizan or mechanic, who only knows that he is descended from the Portuguese, because he speaks the language and bears a name of that race. It has often been a source of much enjoyment to the writer to converse in their own language with some of the old Dutch gentlemen, the relics of a bygone age ; to observe how many of the national characteristics they still retain ; to listen to the traditions and anecdotes of which they are the sole custodians ; and to sympathize with the mingled feeling of pleasure and regret, with which they look back upon a time when they occupied a position of eminence and superiority as the governing body in the island. The younger branches have become more assimilated in thought and feeling with the English. They only know of the past by tradition. Their education has been received in English, in some instances in England ; and with the youthful eye of hope they look forward to distinction under the existing regime. It is unquestionable that they have much talent among them ; that with equal opportunities they are second to none in sharpness and readiness, though not perhaps *as a rule* in depth or solidity ; and that in every walk of life in which any of their members have trodden, whether on the bench or at the bar, in the church or in medicine, they have acquitted themselves well. As clerks they are unrivalled in neatness and accuracy. The dress and habits of life of the better classes resemble those of Europeans. The Dutch language is spoken by but few of the burghers, while strange to say the Portuguese has survived, and is still commonly used in their houses.

The Moormen as they were called by the Portuguese, Dutch, and English successively, have been so long located here as to have lost all connection with the country from whence they originally came, and to justify their being regarded now, as sons of the soil. They are probably the descendants of Arabs who settled in Ceylon and the Indian continent, and intermarried with the native races. Their spoken language is Tamil, although Arabic is taught in all their schools; their religion is Mohamedanism and their occupation trade and barter. They are the most speculative, enterprising and money making of all the natives of the island, and have been called not inaptly, the Jews of the east. In the towns they are hawkers and shop-keepers, and few are the articles they cannot produce or procure for a purchaser. In the interior they penetrate to the remotest villages, carrying with them salt, knives, looking glasses, cloth, brass ware, beads, &c. and bartering them for horns, skins, cotton, grain, coffee, cattle, &c. Their goods are carried about either on the heads or shoulders of men, or on the backs of bullocks in pack saddles. Their habitations are a few talipot leaves, their food a simple meal of rice and curry. Thus they wander from place to place encamping at well known halting stations, and after lighting a fire they lie down to rest. The dawn of day finds them ready to proceed, and the woods ring with their "hu hu" as they drive along their cattle, the sound of whose tinkling brass bells falls pleasantly on the ear as they move slowly on. They also avail themselves of the bright moon-light nights of Ceylon. A pleasant time for travel.

The Englishman shaves his beard and allows his hair

of his head to grow; he uncovers his head to salute a
friend and smiles. The moorman shaves his head and lets
his beard grow; he uncovers his feet and looks grave
when he meets an acquaintance. Moormen generally
wear on the head a white cloth cone-shaped skull cap,
affording but little protection against the sun for their
shaven crowns, which nevertheless they expose with im-
punity to its rays. They are finely made, and their features delicately chiselled. They are inimitable traders,
and generally succeed in getting the best side of a bargain.

RESIDENTS.

The residents in Ceylon as distinguished from the inhabitants, are the Malabar Coolies, the Na'ttucotta chitties,
the Parsees, the Caffres, the Malays, and the Europeans.
The Tamil coolies come over from the eastern or Coro-
mandal coast, principally from the district of Madura.
By them, all the work on the coffee estates is done, except the felling of forest. They are induced to leave
their country by the high wages they receive here. They
periodically revisit their own land and when they have
saved enough they usually cease to return here. Their
habits are simple and their wants few. They are much
better treated, and enjoy more liberty here than under
the company's government. But now that India belongs
to the crown, matters will mend in that respect. Their
religion is Hinduism.

The Na'ttucotta chitties are a very interesting class of
people. They are brokers from India and are engaged
actively in trade. Their fidelity in their transactions used
to be proverbial, and while thousands of rupees pass
through their hands their mode of life is simple in
the extreme. The Parsees are by no means numerous in

Ceylon. They are generally connected with mercantile houses in Bombay, whither their ancestors fled to escape the persecution they underwent in Persia from their own countrymen. They are disciples of Zoroaster and are fire worshippers. Their dress is white with a glazed elevated turban. They are a fine race, and their manners are very pleasing and gentlemanly. They live in great style in Bombay, and generally drive the finest horses. One of their number the late Sir Jamsejee Jijeebhoy of Bombay was created a baronet by the Queen. Here they only remain on account of the demands of business.

The Caffres are the descendants of recruits from the west coast of Africa, many of whom were once slaves under the Portuguese at Goa. They are woolly headed, and have all the characteristics of the Negro. They are either soldiers or pioneers in the road department.

The Malays originally came from the straits of Malacca, and were enrolled in the Ceylon Rifle Regiments. Their descendants are mostly to be found engaged in the military service. They are in religion Mahomedans. Their stature is low, but they are compactly and powerfully made, very brave, and fond of war. Their favourite weapon is a poisoned kris which they use when at close quarters. They are however drilled and dressed in European style, and on parade manœuvre as well as Europeans. The children are educated in the English language and trained to the art of war as early as possible, and they grow up smart intelligent men.

The Europeans are either civil or military servants of Government, or else merchants, planters and tradesmen. Most of them look forward to quitting the island on securing a competency; though this hope too often proves futile. The climate is not unfavorable to health with ordinary prudence and attention to food and drink, and the mountain regions produce specimens of stalwart men, with ruddy countenances and free step, that would do credit to any country.

The missionaries are both Europeans and Americans. They have devoted themselves to the noblest object within the scope of man,—the elevation and salvation of their ignorant brethren. Many of them are located in the peninsula of Jaffna, where several have attained to a good old age; willing to live and die amongst the sons of their adoption, for whose sake many of them have parted for life with those of their own race most dear to them. The subject of missionary labor will however be treated of separately hereafter.

CHAPTER, III.

The Animals, Vegetables, and Minerals of Ceylon.

In a country where the climate, soil, and scenery vary so much as they do in Ceylon, we are prepared to find an equal variety in its animal, vegetable, and mineral productions; and such is indeed the case.

ANIMALS.

The natural history of Ceylon affords a wide field of research for the student. Its vast forests, seldom disturbed save by the hunter, abound with every form of life from the stately elephant, to the blood thirsty musquito. Its seas and rivers team with fish of the most exquisite beauty and the most grotesque form, their colors often rivaling those of the birds and insects that swarm upon its shores.

The principal quadrupeds are the elephant, the buffalo, the elk, the cheeta, the bear, the wild hog, the deer, the porcupine, the monkey, the jackall, the wild cat, the hare, the mongoos, the squirrel, the jerboa, the house rat, and the musk rat.

The principal birds are the eagle, the kite, the hawk, the owl, the devil bird, the crow, the pea fowl, the jungle fowl, the pelican, the flamingo, the crane, the heron, the curlew, the duck, the partridge, the quail, the snipe, the pigeon, the parrot, the woodpecker, the myna, &c.

Amongst sea fish there are the shark, the dolphin, the sea-pig, the porpoise, the seer fish, the mullet, the sole, the sardine, and the rock cod, besides crabs lobsters, shrimps, turtle, &c., &c. In the fresh waters are alligators, eels, water tortoises, and various kinds of fish.

The principal reptiles are iguanas, lizards, snakes, frogs, toads, tarantulas, and centipedes.

Of insects there are butterflies, moths, beetles, grass-hoppers, glow-worms, ants, ticks, musquitos, &c., &c.

It would occupy much more space than our limits can permit, to describe all these creatures; we can speak particularly only of a few.

The elephant is to be met with wherever nature affords him shelter and man's ruthless hand is not raised against his life. He wanders alike in the cold forests of New-era Ellin, or the suffocating jungles of Bintenne. The configuration of the Ceylon, is different from that of the African elephant. None of the females, and very few of the males have tusks. Their height averages about eight feet, though there are instances of their having attained nine feet. When in herds they are peaceful and often timid, more disposed by far, to shun, than to provoke an encounter; but the solitary or rogue elephant is a vindictive, treacherous, and dangerous foe, delight-ing in wanton and unprovoked destruction, and at-tacking his victim at the moment when least prepared for him. The rogue, is always a male; he does not differ in physical conformation from others of his species, and it would appear that he has for some unex-plained reason separated himself, or been separated by the others, from their company; and henceforth his hand is, so to speak, against every one, and every one's hand against him. Elephants are periodically captured in large enclosures, called *Kraals*, a Dutch word, signify-ing a pen. The Moormen also capture them individu-ally, for export to India. When caught, the legs and trunks of the elephants are secured to large trees by strong ropes, when hunger and fatigue soon subdue them, after which they are employed in dragging or lifting heavy burdens, or in adding dignity and grandeur to processions. By their capture, and by the assaults of sportsmen who seek them in the remotest jungles, their numbers are diminishing in many parts of the island.

The buffalo, though a denizen of the forest, has been domesticated, and is commonly used by the natives to plough their fields. At some seasons of the year, they are turned loose, often mixing with their untamed brethren. They however, know the voice of their owner, and though sometimes dangerous to strangers, submit to his rule.

The bear and cheeta roam the forests, and when wounded or apprehensive of being attacked, are sometimes dangerous to man. They are however seldom the aggressors.

The peafowl is a shy and wary bird remarkable for the beautiful plumage of the male ; it is to be met with most commonly in the northern and eastern districts. The jungle fowl resemble our domestic fowl. They are very numerous on the central road leading from Kandy to Jaffna. On seeing man approaching, they retire into the jungle, and reappear when he has passed. The devil bird is so called from the appalling shriek which it often utters in the jungle at night.

Crows are the scavengers of towns ; wherever man takes up his abode, these useful though often annoying birds follow, and in company with the pariah dogs, remove from his vicinity all those impurities which would otherwise breed disease.

During the heavy rains which occur towards the

end of the year, the low grounds in the northern and eastern provinces are converted into sheets of shallow water. These become the haunts of innumerable birds of the wading and swimming order. The pelicans are peculiarly note-worthy, from their remarkable bills which have a capacious pouch attached to them. They live mainly on fish, which they are able to swallow whole.

The alligators which frequent the rivers and lakes, are formidable and dangerous to man. Those which literally swarm in the tanks, are properly crocodiles, and are only dangerous to deer and smaller animals. Snarks are the terror of bathers, and abound all round the island. The sea pig or dugong, is found in the neighborhood of Manaar and bears some fancied resemblance to the mermaid of fable.

Of shells, the varieties are very numerous and beautiful; one species found in the Batticaloe lake is called the musical shell, from the circumstance that on still nights a sound which it is supposed to emit, is heard beneath the surface of the water, resembling the vibrations of a finger glass when the moistened finger is passed round its rim. The pearl oyster is found in largest numbers on the west coast, on banks lying off Aripo to the south of Manaar.

VEGETABLES.

The vegetable productions of Ceylon are as numerous and varied as the animal. The principal trees of value as timber, are the ebony, calamander, satin, jack, halmille, nadille, keena, mendore, del, tulip, teak, and palmira which latter is however a palm.

The principal trees yielding fruit or seed of value to

man either as food or otherwise, are the tamarind, man-go, orange, margosa, elipe, cotton, cashew, bilembe, almond, pumelo, lime, pomegranate, wood apple, lowey lowey, rambotan, gurka, bullock's heart, guava, mul-berry, cinnamon, and coffee.

Among trees yielding shade, and of little other value, the various kinds of banyan are prominent. In the Central Province as we ascend to the higher regions the rhododendrons and tree ferns are among the most strik-ing objects of interest.

Of palms, the talipot, the palmyra, the cocoanut, the arecanut, the kitul, and the sago, are the principal.

Of vegetables, the most common are, the brinjal, pumpkin, bandikai, cucumber, bean, spinach, tomata, sweet potato, yam, &c. The hills produce cauliflowers, cabbages, pease and potatoes, besides various English fruits including the peach and strawberry. In some parts of the low country, and especially in Jaffna, some Eu-ropean vegetables have been cultivated with success, during the cold season.

MINERALS.

Ceylon has always been famous for its mineral pro-ductions : its "sapphires, topazes, amethysts, garnets, and other costly stones" were the theme of travellers, who told moreover of a ruby, belonging to royalty, " a span in length, without a flaw, and brilliant beyond de-scription," (Marco Polo.)

The principal gems of Ceylon, are the amethyst, gar net, ruby, chrysoberyl, sapphire, cinnamon stone, cat's eye, moon stone, and opal. They are sought for with most success, in the neighborhood of Ballangodde, and

Ratnapura, or the city of gems; and are also found at Newera Ellia, in Uva, near Kandy, Matele, and Newera Ellia.

Of metals, gold has been met with, as well as nickel, cobalt, and tellurium,* but in quantities too small to remunerate the search after them. Iron of a very fine quality is plentiful, and nitre and plumbago are abundant in the district of Saffragam, where tin has also been discovered.

Rock crystal, hornblende, mica, hyperstene, feldspar, calcspar, bitterspar, &c. are abundant : iron quartz, manganese, &c. are found in Saffragam and else where.†

---

* Sir E. Tennant.
† Asiatic Society's journal for 1847.

CHAPTER IV.

Historical Sketch.

The history of Ceylon under its ancient kings is contained in a work written in the Pali language in the fifth
century after Christ, by Mahanamo, an uncle of Dha'tu Sena the reigning king. It is divided into two parts respectively denominated the Mahawanse, and the Suluwanse.
The Mahawanse, or "great dynasty," embraces the
period between B. C. 543, and A. D. 301, and was compiled from the annals then existing, in the vernacular
language.* The Suluwanse, or "lesser dynasty" carries
on the history to A. D. 1,758, the whole work compris-
ing a period of no less than twenty three centuries. Its
translation into English was commenced by the Hon.
G. Turnour, Esq. of the Ceylon civil service; and
though death interrupted his labors, he lived long enough
to complete the first thirty-eight chapters of one of the
most remarkable and authentic ancient records in existence.

In designating it an authentic record however, we
must be understood to speak in a modified sense. When
we find it related for instance, that the island was originally inhabited by demons, we infer that the aborigines
were devil worshippers. Again, when we are told that
amongst many other cures which a certain king effected,
he drew forth a snake from the stomach of a man who
had long been incommoded by this troublesome tenant,
by fastening a piece of meat to a string and placing it
as a bait in the patient's throat, we come to the conclu-
sion that the king devoted himself to the study of med-

* Turnour's introduction to the Mahawanse.

cine and surgery, and was a successful practitioner. On the other hand, the wars in which the island was engaged, the public works undertaken, the dates assigned to their construction, &c., &c., these as recorded in this work, appear worthy of all credit.* It would be of little practical use, and far beyond our limits to dwell on the history of each individual sovereign who has in turn appeared upon the stage of life. Some there were who left lasting mementos—either for good or ill,—of their existence: of these we shall speak more particularly: others there were whose lives were unmarked by any acts worthy of note; these we shall but briefly allude to, or pass by in silence. A complete list of the one hundred and sixty-five sovereigns who successively filled the throne will be found annexed, framed on the basis of the one originally drawn out by Turnour: and those who are desirous of more minute particulars than this little work affords, are referred to the Mahawanse, the Rajaratnacari, and the Rajavali, as well as to the Tamil epic poem called the Ramayana.

Our subject will be divided in these pages, into three parts;—the Mahawanse, or great dynasty; the Suluwanse, or lesser dynasty; the Tamils; and the European occupation.

* "After the most minute examination of the portion of the Mahawanse compiled by Mahanamo, I am fully prepared to certify that I have not met with any other passage in the work, connected with religion and its superstitions, than those already noticed, which could by the most sceptical be considered as prejudicial to its historical authenticity." (*Turnour's introduction to the Mahawanse.*) The exceptions made by Turnour have reference to the date assigned for the landing of Wijeyo in the island: it is believed by some that it took place B. C. 477 instead of B. C. 543. L. L.

THE MAHAWANSE, OR GREAT DYNASTY.

In the sixth century before Christ, there reigned in La'la, a principality of Magadha, or as it is now called Bahar, in the valley of the Ganges, a king named Singha, or Siha bahu, who was said to have been descended from a lion. He was also of the illustrious race of Suriavas who claimed as their progenitor a beneficent Being, who came down from the sun, and taught mankind the arts of civilized life. Wijayo the eldest son of this king, was so lawless and unruly a character that his father was eventually compelled to dismiss him from his court. Collecting together a band of kindred spirits, Wijayo set sail in search of adventure, and ultimately reached Ceylon and landed on its shores in the neighborhood of what is now called Putlam. He found the island inhabited by a rude uncivilized people, whose origin is involved in obscurity, and who worshipped snakes and devils, and were consequently called Na'gas, and Yakkos.

Marrying a Yakko Princess, Wijayo established himself at Tamena Newera, not far from the place of his landing; and having by the aid of his wife obtained the mastery of the island, he repudiated the alliance, dismissed her and her children, married the daughter of an Indian Prince, invited over from the Continent, merchants and artizans; located his followers in different parts of the country, the better to develop its resources; and laid the foundation, of its future greatness, giving to it the name of his father, Singha.

Dying without issue, his nephew Panduwa'sa succeeded him, and pursued the same line of policy as his predecessor. He married a relative of Gotama Budha, and in order to spread civilization encouraged the brothers of his queen, who came over with her from the continent, to found subordinate principalities, which were however subject to himself and his successors as the paramount sovereigns of the whole island; a fact it will be well to bear in mind in perusing this work.

It was during this reign, that Ceylon was subdivided into three parts. " All to the north of the Mahawelliganga was comprised in the denomination Pihiti, or the Raja-ratta, from its containing the ancient capital and the residence of royalty; south of this was Rahano or Rohuna, bounded on the east and south by the sea, and by the Mahawelliganga and Kaluganga on the north and west; a portion of this division near Tangallo still retains the name of Roona. The third was the Maya-ratta which lay between the mountains, the two great rivers and the sea, having the Dedera Oya to the north, and the Kaluganga as its southern limit."*

Panduwa'sa established himself at Anuradhapura, so called from Anuradha its founder, and there constructed the first of those vast tanks which subsequently became so numerous, and which testify to this day to the efforts conde—and as it appears with so much success, to develope the rich agricultural resources of a country which under the aborigines had laid uncultivated. For the space of the following two hundred years, more attention appears to have been devoted to agriculture and improvement, than to religion. The succession to the crown

---

(Sir E. T.) From other passages in the same work on Ceylon it appears that both Adam's Peak and Kandy were included in Maya-ratta; it is therefore scarcely correct to say that it lay between the *mountains,* the two great rivers, and the sea.

was on the death of Panduwa'sa, the subject of dispute, and ultimately Pandukabhayo, by the aid of the aborigines or Yakkos, succeeded in placing himself upon the throne. He built several tanks and divided the island into village settlements.

In the year B. C. 307 King Tisso, or as he is called De'wa'nan pia tisso or "Tisso, the delight of the Deities," ascended the throne. Having dispatched an embassy entrusted with valuable gifts, to Dharmmaso'ka, the king of Magadha, that sovereign in return sent his son Mahindo, to inculcate the doctrines of Budhism in Ceylon; which with the aid of his sister Sanghamitta, he succeeded in doing, (B. C. 267.) At the urgent request of the Singhalese king, a branch of the Bo tree under which Gotama attained the Budhaship, was with much pomp brought over from Magadha, and planted at Anuradhapura, where it continues to flourish to this day, after the lapse of 2,000 years. The energy which had heretofore been expended mainly on agricultural works, now took a new direction, though not entirely.diverted from its former channel; and from this period dates the erection of those stupendous masses of masonry about Anuradhapura and other ancient cities, which Singhalese kings vied with each other in constructing. The earliest of these Dagobas, as they are called, were erected by king Tisso, whose name has consequently been handed down to posterity amidst the plaudits of the historian. The three cousins of the king who successively filled the throne, followed in his foot-steps, and during the century immediately ensuing on his death, the number of Wiharis and Dagobas rapidly increased, though it is but just to add, that the number of tanks increased also.

During the reign of Suratissa, the last of the three cousins, two Malabar adventures, Sena and Gootika by name, who had been respectively entrusted with military and naval command, turned their arms against the sovereign to whom they had pledged themselves and usurped his throne. (B. C. 237.) After a reign of twenty-two years, they were deposed and killed by Asela, a member of the royal family, and the crown reverted to its rightful owners. It would have been well had they taken warning by this event; but the people being better suited to an agricultural, than to a military life, it had become customary to employ Tamil mercenaries in the military service; and in course of time the superior energy and bravery of that people proved highly dangerous to the supremacy of the Singhalese race. Ten years after the restoration of that dynasty Elala a prince of Tanjore invaded the island, slew the reigning king, and ascended the vacant throne; it is however due to the usurper to add, that on the testimony of his enemies he is said to have " administered justice with impartiality to friends and foes." A bell was suspended by his bed side, which all those who had any grievances to redress, and desired an audience, were at liberty to ring.

At the end of forty-four years, Dutugaimunu, a descendant of the deposed king, encountered Elala on the field of battle and engaged him in single combat. After a conflict in which equal bravery was displayed on both sides, the elephants on which the rival princes were mounted closed with each other, and that of Elala falling in the charge, crushed his rider to death. The generous conqueror caused a monument to be erected on the spot where his brave adversary had fallen

and decreed that in future even royalty itself should not
pass the locality without testifying its respect for his
memory. The Mahawanse records that " on reaching the
quarter of the city in which it stands, it has been the custom for the monarchs of Lanka to silence their music,
whatsoever procession they may be heading;" and it is
related on the authority of Forbes, that when the pro-
tender to the throne was escaping from pursuit after the
rebellion of 1818, he descended from his palanquin on
approaching the place, " and although weary and almost
incapable of exertion, not knowing the precise spot, he
continued on foot till assured that he had passed far beyond the ancient memorial."*

On his accession to the throne after the death of Elala,
Dutugaimunu commenced the construction of the great
Ruanwelli dagoba at Anuradhapura, the remains of
which exist to this day. A large number of the aborigines
or Yakkos, who were employed in its construction, are
said to have been converted to Budhism during their sojourn in the capital. Dutugaimunu, amongst many other
acts of liberality, constructed and embellished the famous
brazen palace, as a residence for the priests. His name
has consequently been blazoned on the scroll of fame,
in the annals of his country. He died B. C. 187, and
on his decease disputes arose about the order of succession, during which the priesthood succeeded in adding
considerably to their importance by throwing the weight
of their influence into the one scale or the other. In the
year B. C., 104, Walagambahu 1st ascended the throne,
but he had scarcely done so before a successful inroad
from the Indian coast, conducted by seven Tamil kings

* Forbes—as quoted by Sir E. Tennent.

compelled him to seek refuge in the vicinity of Adam's
Peak, while the victors took possession of Anuradhapura, a considerable part of the spoils of the richly endowed city, and one of the wives of the king, being sent as
trophies, to the Dekkan. At the end of fifteen years,
the deposed sovereign succeeded in recovering his throne
and his queen; events " which he commemorated in the
usual manner by the erection of dagobas, tanks and
wiharis."* It was under the auspices of this king
that the oral discourses of Budha, as handed down
by tradition, were reduced to writing by priests appointed for the purpose, (B. C. 89,) in a cave temple near
Matele called the Alu-wihari, which is still in existence.

In the year B. C. 47, we meet with the first instance of
a woman assuming the reins of government. They were
seized by " the infamous Anula," as she is designated
in the Mahawanse, after having poisoned both her hus-
band and her son. Her subsequent career is one cata-
logue of iniquity and crime; and her death was eventually brought about by the son of that son whom she had
caused to be made away with. His name was Makalan-
tisso: and after ascending the throne he enclosed the
city of Anuradhapura by a stone wall sixty-four miles
in circuit, and ten and a half feet wide: he died B. C.
19.

During the two following centuries little that is worthy
of note occurs in the history of the island; one episode
may however be mentioned, as a warning to " merry
monarchs." King Yasa Siloo, or Yatalakatissa ascended
the throne A. D. 52, after having put an end to his eld-
er brother the reigning king. " There was a young gate-

* Sir E. Tennant.

porter" (says the Mahawanse,) "the son of the porter
Datto, named Subho, who in person strongly resembled
the raja. The monarch Yassalako (Yatalakatissa) in a
merry mood having decked out the said Subho the messenger in the vestments of royalty, and seated him on
the throne, putting the livery bonnet of the messenger
on his own head, stationed himself at a palace gate with
the porter's staff in his hand. While the ministers of
state were bowing down to him who was seated on the
throne, the raja was enjoying the deception. He was in
the habit from time to time of indulging in these scenes.
On a certain day (when the farce was repeated,) address-
ing himself to the merry monarch, the messenger ex-
claimed 'how does that balattho dare to laugh in my
presence;' and succeeded in getting the king put to
death. The porter Subho thus usurped the sovereignty,
and administered it for six years, under the title of
Subho."

In the year of our Lord 209, and in the first year of the
reign of king Wairatissa, famed for his thorough acquaintance "with the principles of justice and equity," (Mahawanse;) a schism occurred among the Budhists, called
the We'tullian heresy. Violent, and apparently successful efforts were made to suppress it; but on prince Mahasen being exalted to the throne A. D. 276, he publicly professed his adherence to the tenets of the hereti-
cal party, their doctrines having been secretly taught
him by one of the schismatics. He next proceeded to
mutilate the brazen palace which had been used as a
residence of the priests, and introduced various innovations into the forms of worship previously observed. His
proceedings gave rise to a revolt, during which his fa-

structor was assasinated; whereon the apostate king, either really, or apparently convinced of his errors, re- turned to the bosom of the faith he had sought to destroy, and employed himself during the remainder of his life in the design and construction of magnificent public works. He died A. D. 275, and with him ends the "great dynasty." "The sovereigns of the Suluwanse who followed, were no longer of the unmixed blood, but the offspring of parents, only one of whom was descend- ed from the sun, and the other from the bringer of the Bo-tree, or the sacred tooth ; on that account, because the god Sakkraia had ceased to watch over Ceylon, because piety had disappeared, and the city of Anuradhapura was in ruins, and because the fertility of the land was di- minished, the kings who succeeded Mahasen were no longer reverenced as of old."[*]

THE SULUWANSE OR LESSER DYNASTY.

"The story of the kings of Ceylon of the *Suluwanse* or lower line, is but a narrative of the decline of the power and prosperity which had matured under the Bengal conquerors, and of the rise of the Malabar ma- rauders, whose ceaseless forays and incursions eventual- ly reduced authority to feebleness, and the island to de- solation. The vapid biography of the royal imbeciles who filled the throne from the third to the thirteenth century, scarcely embodies an incident of sufficient in- terest to diversify the monotonous repetition of temples founded and dagobas repaired, of tanks constructed and priests endowed with lands reclaimed and fertilized by the " forced labor" of the subjugated races. Civil dis-

---

[*] Extract from the Rajavali as quoted by Sir E. Tennent.

sensions, religious schisms, royal intrigues and assassin-
ations, contributed equally with foreign invasions to diminish the influence of the monarchy and exhaust the
strength of the kingdom."

" Of sixty-two sovereigns who reigned from the death
of Mahasen, A. D. 301, to the accession of Prakrama
Bahu, A. D. 1153, nine met a violent death at the hands
of their relatives or subjects, two ended their days in exile, one was slain by the Malabars, and four committed
suicide. Of the lives of the larger number, the Budhist
historians fail to furnish any important incidents; they
relate merely the merit which each acquired by his liberality to the national religion or the more substantial
benefits conferred on the people by the formation of lakes
for irrigation."* Such is the account given by the elo-
quent writer to whom we have already so often referred, of the kings of the lesser dynasty.

It was during the reign of Kitsiri Maiwan the first,
the successor of Mahasen, that the relic supposed to be
the right canine tooth of Gotama Budha was conveyed
to the island by a Brahman princes of Kalinga A. D.
298, and deposited by the king himself " in a casket of
great purity made of ' phalika stone,' and lodged in the
edifice called the Dhammachakko, built by Dewa'na'npi-
atisso" (Mahawanse, p. 241.) Budhadaso who ascended
the throne, A. D. 339, is described as being " a mine
of virtues and an ocean of riches." It was this monarch
who is said to have performed the wonderful cure on the
man who had a snake in his stomach. He composed
the work Saratthasangaho, still consulted by Singhalese
medical practitioners, and "ordained that there should

* Sir E. Tennent.

be a physician for every twice five villages on the main road, for the reception of the crippled, deformed, and destitute ; he built asylums in various places, provided with the means of subsisting these objects." (Mahawanse.)

About the middle of the fifth century after Christ, the marauders from the Malabar coast once more succeeded in making themselves masters of the Singhalese capital. They were however expelled by Dhatu Sena a prince of the royal blood who ascended the throne A. D. 459, re-assembled the fugitive citizens, and directed his energies to the restoration of agricultural works and the repair of the sacred buildings. He was deposed by his nephew, whose mother the king had caused to be burnt, and prince Kasyapa was exalted to the throne. This unnatural son, after having subjected his father to a series of cruel indignities which he bore with the utmost magnanimity, put an end to his life by embedding him within a wall of masonry. He next attempted to compass the destruction of his brother, who succeeded however in making his escape. The royal parricide sought, but sought in vain, to stifle the agonies of remorse by deeds of charity and the erection of magnificent structures ; the ministers of religion refused to accept his gifts, and he was forced to offer them in the name and by means of third parties. Apprehensive of retribution, he fortified the rock Sigiri in the district of Matele, and thither he removed himself and his treasure. After an exile of eighteen years his brother Mogallano returned to the island from India, with an army he had succeeded in raising there, and the two brothers met in mortal conflict at Ambhatakolo in the Seven Korles. The head of the usurper was struck off by the avenging sword of his brother, and the conqueror at once marched upon the capital, assumed the reins of government A. D. 495, and died after a reign of eighteen years, during which he organized a naval force to repel the incursions of the Tamils, and signalized his rule by many acts of beneficence.

The murder of Dhatu Sena forms the subject of the thirty-eighth chapter of the Mahawanse, the last one translated by the accomplished Turnour; Mahanamo, the writer of the original work, was the relative and personal friend of the king whose death he has recorded; and after relating how the usurper embedded his father "exposing his face only to the east" he adds,—"what wise man after being informed of this, would covet riches, life, or prosperity!" and again,—"Thus the ten kings (mentioned in this chapter) who were pre-eminently endowed with prosperity, (nevertheless) appeared in the presence of death in a state of destitution. The wise man seeing that in the riches of the wealthy there is no stability, will cease to covet riches."

Of the eight kings who reigned between A. D. 515 and 586, "two died by suicide, three by murder, and one by grief occasioned by the treason of his son." "During a period of such violence and anarchy persons in dustry was suspended and extensive emigration took place to Bahar and Orissa." (Sir E. T.) Amongst other acts of violence king Sanghatissa was murdered by his prime-minister, who in his turn fell by the hands of the people of Rohuna during a revolt which took place in a time of famine. In the civil wars that prevailed, Tamil mercenaries were as usual employed on one side or the other. On one occasion however they were defeated and a number made prisoners who were distributed as slaves amongst the various temples in the island. We find nevertheless that the history of Ceylon between the 9th and 11th centuries is made up of the acts of the Malabars, more than of the native kings. " They filled every office including that of prime minister; and they decided the claims of competing candidates for the crown." Finding at length that their exclusion from Anuradhapura, where they had located themselves in considerable numbers, was impossible, the reigning king Agrabodhi 4th in the 8th century removed the seat of government to Pollonnarua; " where tanks and palaces surpassing in beauty, and dagobas nearly equalling in size, those of the ancient capital, were constructed." (Sir E. Tennent.)

In the year 858, we read of " the first foreign expedition deliberately undertaken by Singhalese." Its object was to aid the son of the king of Pandia (or Madura) in a war against his father, who a few years previously had overrun both the ancient and modern capitals of the island, and been bought off by a heavy ransom. The expedition was successful and a large amount of plunder was brought back from Madura. In 954, the Singhalese and Pandian kings jointly engaged in a war with the king of Chola. (Tanjore.) The allies were defeated and the Pandian king was forced to take refuge in Ceylon. Engaging in a conspiracy against his protector, he was expelled from the island without being permitted to carry away his regalia. These the Cholian king demanded, and on their being refused brought over an invading army to Ceylon, which was defeated by the inhabitants of Rohuna.

In the year 997, king Mahindo married a princess of
Kalinga, (the northern circars of the Madras Presidency.)
During the reign of his son who succeeded him, a rebellion broke out in which a Tamil army supported the
royalists against the insurgents.   "The island was now
reduced to the extreme of anarchy and insecurity ; 'the
foreign population' had increased to such an extent as
to gain a complete ascendancy over the native inhabitants, and the sovereign had lost authority over both."

"In A. D. 1023, the Cholians again invaded Ceylon,
carried the king captive to the coast of India, (where he
died in exile,) and established a Malabar viceroy at Pollonnarua, who had possession of the island for nearly
thirty years, protected in his usurpations by a foreign
army.   Thus 'throughout the reign of nineteen kings'
says the Rajaratnacari, ' extending over eighty-six years,
the Malabars kept up a continual war with the Singhalese, till they filled by degrees every village in the island."   (Sir E. Tennent.)

Whilst this was the state of things at the capital, matters were little better in the principality of Rohuna,
where the royal family still maintained the semblance
of sovereignty.   Four brothers contended for the tottering throne, and each in succession fell from it again
after a brief reign; until in the year 1071, the minister
Lokiswera assumed it, and held his Court at Kattegam,
on the borders of the Badulla and Humbantotte district.
His name is only recorded on account of his being the
progenitor of a prince who effected the deliverance of
the island, restored order and industry, and for a brief
period recalled to mind the glories of the " Great Dynasty."

On the death of Lokiswera, his son Wijayo Bahu who succeeded him, followed by the mountaineers of Rohuna, delivered the capital from the Tamils, organized a standing army to guard the coasts, and received deputations from beyond the seas. On his death a civil war for the succession ensued, which terminated in the accession, by the choice of the people, of the young prince Prakrama, whose accomplishments were of the most varied as well as comprehensive character, many of them having been acquired at foreign courts. He was crowned king of Pihiti at Pollonnarua, A. D. 1153, and subsequently on the subjugation of Rohuna which had for sometime continued refractory, " Sole king of Lanka."

" There is no name in Singhalese history," says Sir E. Tennent, " which holds the same rank in the admiration of the people as that of Prakrama Bahu, since to the piety of Devinipiatissa he united the chivalry of Dutugaimunu." He rebuilt the Budhist temples, " and covered the face of the kingdom with works of irrigation to an extent that would seem incredible did not their existing ruins corroborate the historical narrative of his stupendous labors." So great had been the decay of Budhism under the dominion of the Tamils that only five ordained priests were to be found in the island : an embassy was therefore sent to Arramana or Siam where the Budhist religion prevailed, for the ordination of additional priests. While however the new king was devoting himself to the interests of Budhism, the restoration of order, and the arts of peace, he did not neglect those of war. Some merchants of Ceylon having been plundered by subjects of the king of Cambodia and Arramana in the Siamese peninsula, he sent forth an expedition

under the command of a Tamil leader to punish the outrage ; which successfully accomplished its object. He
next turned his arms against the Cholian and Pandian
kings who had assisted the Tamils against the island, whom
he defeated, and made tributary to him; annexed the
island of Ramesuram and the adjacent coast of India to
his kingdom ; founded a city in the Pandian dominions;
and after commemorating his victory by the coining of
money, returned in triumph to Ceylon.

. Prakrama Bahu died A. D. 1186, and with him ends
the glory of Ceylon under its native rulers. For the
thirty years that ensued, the island was a prey to the
anarchy occasioned by the struggles of rival claimants
to the crown, who in rapid succession ascended it only
to be hurled down again, their reigns being with two
exceptions calculated by days and months instead of
years. In the year 1211, an adventurer from the
northern circars, Ma'gha by name, landed with a force
of twenty four thousand men and made himself master
of all Ceylon ; his government was signalized by cruelty,
oppression, and wanton destruction ; and to use the words
of the Mahawanse, " the whole island was like a house
set on fire, the Demilos plundering it from village to
village." After the lapse of twenty years, a member of
the royal family succeeded in recovering those parts of
the island called Maya and Rohuna, and established himself at Jambudronha or Dambedinia fifty miles north of
Colombo, where he reigned under the designation of
Wijayo Bahu 3d. A. D. 1235. The invaders continued
however to hold possession of the capital and the districts about it, which they secured from attack by a line
of forts extending from Pollonnarua to the sea coast on
the west.

Pandita Prakrama Bahu next ascended the throne A. D. 1266, and succeeded in wresting a further portion of the island from the invaders. He encouraged learning and improved the internal communication between different places by the construction of roads and bridges. During his reign the island was successively invaded by the Malays and the Tamils; but their incursions were successfully repelled. It was by this king that the sacred tooth called the delada relic was removed to Kandy, or as it was then called, Sriwardenepura. On his death the repeated attacks of its Tamil enemies left Ceylon but little time for rest In the year 1303, the city of Yapahu in the Seven Korles became the capital; but the Pandian invaders soon followed, plundered the city, and carried off the sacred tooth to India. The unhappy sovereigns transferred the seat of Government to Kurnegalle, then to Gampola, next to Peredinia, and eventually to Jaya-wardhanapura, or as it is now called, Kotta, the Singhalese word *Kotuwe*, a fort. having probably been adopted by the Portuguese on their arrival as the name of the place, from ignorance of its meaning. Five years previous to this last removal of the capital, an event occurred which the Singhalese chronicles have passed over in silence, but which the diligence of Sir E. Tennent has brought to light. So early as the fourth century after Christ, friendly intercourse had been established between the island of Ceylon and the empire of China, occasioned by the desire of the latter to extend its commerce, and strengthened by the bond of a common religion, Some of the ambassadors sent to Ceylon, recorded on their return to their own country what things they had seen and heard; and these annals are an interesting and

valuable corroboration of the statements in the Mahawanse. In the year 1410 however, a Chinese ambassador entrusted with offerings to Budha, was treacherous-
ly waylaid by Wijayo Bahu 6th, the reigning king of
Ceylon, and escaped with difficulty to his ships. The
position of Ceylon towards China, had previously been
that of deference and recognition of superiority ; and the
emperor, determined to avenge this indignity, dispatched
a naval and military force to Ceylon, which seized the
capital, and carried off the offending king a captive to
China, along with the rest of the royal family. They
were however allowed to return to their own country
on the condition of their paying an annual tribute to
China : the emperor further ordaining that the offending
king should be deposed and the wisest member of the
family exalted to the throne in his stead. The choice
fell on Prakrama Bahu 6th, who with his successors continued to be tributary to China until A. D. 1448.

We have now reached that period in the history of
Ceylon, when the European appears upon the stage. Before proceeding further therefore we shall turn our attention to that part of the island which is at present occupied by the Tamils, and enquire under what circumstances they became located there, and what was the relative position of the Singhalese and Tamil races in Ceylon
at the period of which we are about to speak.

THE TAMILS.

The materials for this part of our subject are far from
being so copious as those from which the rest of this history is compiled. The Mahawanse is essentially a court
chronicle ; it dwells mainly on the annals of the Singhalese kings ; and its writer, who evidently regarded the

Tamils as a horde of ruthless marauders, passes by them and their doings in silence except when they force themselves irresistibly and too often unpleasantly on his notice.

We have already seen how this active and energetic people wedged themselves in amongst the Gangetic race, rendering themselves at the same time indispensable and dangerous. In the course of years they had permeated the whole community and secured a footing from which it was difficult, if not impossible to displace them. In the army and navy they filled the most important stations ; in the state their counsels prevailed ; and in trade and commerce they were the moving spirits. If even at the seat of royalty their presence had become so inconvenient, and their influence so powerful as to lead to the abandonment of the magnificent capital of Anuradhapura with all its splendid monuments and all its traditionary glory, there is little difficulty in understanding how in the remote and less wealthy northern peninsula they would establish themselves without molestation, and how their position there, so near their own country, would afford such facilities for strengthening their numbers, as to enable them eventually, when the Singhalese power had become considerably impaired, to throw off even the semblance of allegiance and assume an independent position.

It has previously been shown that after the removal of the capital from Pollanarua to Dambedinia all the district of Pihiti was filled with Tamils, who drew a line of forts across their southern frontier behind which they thought themselves secure ; and we have also seen how during the commotions which racked the island between A. D. 523, and A. D. 618, "extensive emigrations

took place to Bahar and Orissa." With the further
diminution of the Singhalese, a large portion of
whom doubtless followed the retiring footsteps of royalty,
it is easy to understand how the ancient works for irrigation, the up-keep of which was so essential to agricultural prosperity, would fall into decay ; for the invaders
had always manifested a disposition to appropriate the
treasures which had already been amassed, rather than
to provide for securing permanent benefits which being
prospective they might not remain to enjoy. Thus by
degrees the forest would again encroach upon the former haunts of men ; sickness induced by rank vegetation
and stagnant water would further reduce the numbers
of those who remained in the neighborhood ; and the sur-
vivors would be attracted to where larger and newly
formed communities gave them a more congenial place
of abode. In the choice of their new residence, it is not
unnatural to suppose that the Singhalese would direct
their steps towards the south and west, whither their
monarchs had preceeded them ; that the Tamils would
draw off to the east and north, where a sovereign of their
own nation already swayed an independent sceptre ;
and that the remnant of the aborigines which still retain-
ed their original characteristics and had not intermarried
with the other races, would retire to the forests of Bintenne, where they could pursue unmolested that course
of life they best enjoyed. Thus the once splendid capitals and the fertile regions which surrounded them would
fall a prey to the silent and stealthy inroads of decay,—
inroads, less obtrusive, but not less fatal than those
of the marauders who had periodically dispoiled them
before.

The northern peninsula was in former times known among the Tamils by the name of Manilka'du or the sandy jungle; it was called Na'ga Dwi'pe by the Singhalese because it was occupied by the Na'ga race; and a temple dedicated to Na'ga Tambira'n the god of snakes, still exists in the island of Nynati'vu, where a number of cobras are it is said kept alive and fed by the Panda'rums.

According to the Kyla'sama'lai (a Tamil poem composed by one Veiya of Naloor, about three hundred years ago,) a princess of the Chola race, who suffered from some disease or deformity, was directed to proceed to the northern peninsula of Ceylon, and to bathe in a sacred spring which there existed. Landing in the vicinity of Kangeysontorre, she was met by a devotee who had been born with the face of a mongoos, but had been cured of the defect by bathing in the holy spring, and who had thereupon located himself on a neighboring hill to which he gave the name of Keeremalai or the mongoos mountain. Encouraged by this, the princess also bathed and was cured; and in grateful commemoration of the event she is said to have built the temple of Mavitiapuram which signifies "the town where the horse galloped;" with which is connected the popular legend that she labored under the deformity of having a horse's head, instead of "the human face divine." The princess next proceeded, as the poem relates, to bathe in another sacred spring at a place it calls Kathera'mum near Kyrly: where one Narasingha raja, who is not identified with any sovereign of Ceylon, led an army against her, and after having made her prisoner, married her. The fruits of this union were a son and daughter, and

eventually the grandson of the princess bestowed the
peninsula of Jaffna upon a blind musician from Madura
called Ya'lpa'nan, as a reward for his skill. The newly endowed prince gave the name of Ya'lpa'nam to his
territory, by which name it is known to this day among
the natives, and of which Jaffna is a corruption; he encouraged his countrymen to come over and settle in it,
and on his death a prince of Madura was invited to accept the vacant throne, B. C. 101. This date, the first
we find given, nearly corresponds with that of the invasion of the island by seven Tamil kings, which has already been alluded to, when Waligam Bahu 1st was compelled to flee from his capital. Singha Ariyan, the new
king of Jaffna, generally called Koolankai Chakravarte
or the "deformed armed emperor," erected a palace at
Naloor, the site of which is still pointed out where
an ancient gate-way faces the high road from Jaffna to
Point Pedro, between the second and third mile-stones.
He availed himself of the troubled state of the island to
extend his authority over the Wanny, Manaar, and Mantotte, strengthened his position by fortifying his fron-
tiers, and encouraged immigration from India. Little is
known of the state of things in the north from this period
to the thirteenth century; it is however believed by
many that during that period Mantotte, or as it was called by the Singhalese, Mahatotte "the great ferry," near
the island of Manaar, was the renowned emporium of
the extensive trade carried on between Greece, Rome,
Persia, Arabia, Hindustan, and China, where merchants
from those various countries displayed their wares, and
exchanged them for those not to be procured nearer
home. This opinion is however discountenanced by

Sir E. Tennent who believes Galle to have been the far famed mart of Ceylon : be that as it may, there are grounds for supposing that Mantotte was an important, if not the most important place of commerce ; and it is said that Roman coins of the reigns of Claudius and the Antonines, and the foundations of what appears to have been a Roman building, have in modern times been discovered there.

In the year of our Lord 1303, we find the king of Jaffna in command of an army composed of his own forces and those which his ally the king of Madura had sent over to attack the Singhalese king then reigning at Yapahoo in the Seven Korles. The expedition was successful, and the delada relic was taken by the victors and sent to India. In 1371, another army under the command of "the king of the Ceylonese Malabars," (Mahawanse,) succeeded in taking possession of, and building forts at, Colombo, Negombo, and Chilaw, and "collected tribute from the high and low countries and likewise from the nine ports."* In the year 1410, the Singhalese king, then reigning at Kotta, sent an army against Jaffna, commanded by his son Sapoomal Kuma're, who inflicted much damage on the Tamil territories. Repeating the attack not long after, the young prince, mounted on a fiery charger, advanced upon the northern capital, and after a desperate conflict, the streets running with blood, succeeded in capturing the king, whom he deprived of life : his family was carried captive to the

* See an interesting article on the history of Jaffna by the late Dare Chitty, Esq., in the Asiatic Society's journal, from which several of the facts above recorded have been drawn. There are however one or two discrepancies between what is stated in the Kylasama'lai, and what that gentleman has related, which have been rectified in these pages.

south, and the prince was appointed ruler of the con-
quered provinces as a reward for his prowess.

Before the arrival of the Portuguese however, the
Tamils appear to have regained their liberty ; and a
treaty of amity cemented by inter-marriage, had for
some time been in existence between the kings of the
two races.   From this period the chronicles of both will
be found intermingled with the narrative of the Europeans and their doings.

THE EUROPEAN OCCUPATION.

The. Portuguese.

" And now it came to pass that in the Christian year
1552 in the month of April, a ship from Portugal arrived at Colombo, and information was brought to the king,
(Dharma Prakrama 9th,) that there were in the harbor
a race of very white and beautiful people, who wear
boots and hats of iron, and never stop in one place. They
eat a sort of white stone, and drink blood: and if they
get a fish they give two or three ride in gold for it : and
besides, they have guns with a noise louder than thunder,
and a ball shot from one of them, after traversing a league,
will break a castle of marble."*   Such were the terms
in which the arrival of the Portuguese was announced
to the king of Ceylon. The hats and boots of iron were
part of the armor in which soldiers were in those days
clad, and the stone and blood they were said to eat and
drink were ship biscuit and wine.

The Portuguese Captain Vasco de Gama having in
the year 1498 doubled the Cape of Good Hope, eventu-

---

* The Rajavali as quoted by Sir E. Tennent.

ally landed and formed a settlement at Calicut on the western coast of India. Seven years later, Lorenzo de Almeyda sailed from that place and touched at Point de Galle; and twelve years subsequently, Lopez Soarez the third of the "viceroys of India" as the Portuguese already designated their commanders in the east, resolved to send an expedition to Ceylon.

The supremacy of the Singhalese king over the island had by this time become a shadow. The north of Ceylon was under the Government of a Tamil sovereign: the chiefs of Uva, Peredinia, Mahagam, &c, ruled in their respective provinces as independent princes, their recognition of the once paramount king being merely nominal: the districts of Newerckalawa and the Wanny were held by petty governors professing allegiance either to the Tamil or the Singhalese king, but virtually doing as they pleased: and the "Moormen," who had established themselves in formidable numbers on the sea coasts, and who were the most active and enterprising people in the island, exercised a very important influence over the councils of the kings of Kotta: the construction and upkeep of agricultural works had almost entirely ceased, and already the once fruitful island of Ceylon had become in a great degree dependent on India for rice.

The design already formed by the Portuguese, was to build a fort at Colombo, in order to secure a favorable halting place between Goa and their newly acquired possessions in the spice country of Malacca. Their right to settle there they founded on a promise which they alleged to have been made to Almeyda at Galle, which promise had subsequently been ratified by a letter from the king of Kotta, though in the first instance given

without his sanction.   Alarmed however at the military
character of the new settlement, the king demurred to
the proceedings of the foreigners, but was gained over
by the tempting promises of pecuniary advantage to be
derived from trade, and the hope of military aid against
his domestic enemies : the fort was built,—and the fate
of the island was sealed.   The more astute Moormen
succeeded however in re-awakening the apprehensions
of the king, who encouraged them to make an attack upon the interlopers ; but timely succours arriving
from India, the seige was raised, and the king compelled to acknowledge himself a vassal of Portugal, and to
pay an annual tribute to that power.   In 1520 however,
the Portuguese again provoked an attack by the attempt
to strengthen their position still further, and for some
time their condition was one of extreme danger ; but reinforcements from India once more turned the scales in
their favor ; and the unhappy king, constantly menaced
with attacks from the petty princes in the interior, and
living almost within reach of the Portuguese guns at
Colombo, saw no alternative but to propitiate the foreigners he found himself too weak to expel, and to avail himself of their aid to subdue the unruly spirit of his own
vassals. An alliance, offensive and defensive, was accordingly entered into between the king and the Portuguese ;
but this measure at once roused the angry feelings of the
hardy Kandians, always jealous of foreign intrusion ;
and Maaya Dunnai, the youngest son of the king, already
displeased at an attempt made by his father to alter the
line of succession to the crown, was so disgusted at what
he regarded an act of pusillanimity, that he raised the
standard of revolt, and after causing the king to be as-

sassinated, placed the next legitimate heir upon the
throne, reserving to himself the principality of Setawakka, and securing for his brother that of Raygam. But
the new king manifested a spirit as subservient as that
of his father; and a series of conflicts ensued, in which
the intrepid Maaya Dunnai aided by the Moormen, ever
the bitter foes of the Portuguese, and by succours from
the Zamoran of Calicut, was always foremost in the field,
while the king of Kotta was strenuously supported by
the Europeans; and to ensure their recognition of the
claims of his son to the tottering throne, Bhuwaneka the
7th, the reigning sovereign, consented to send a golden
effigy of his intended successor to Portugal, together
with a richly jewelled crown, which was with much ceremony placed on the head of the image at Lisbon, A. D.
1541; and the name of Don Juan was at the same time
given to the prince, who had previously been known by
that of Dharmapala Bahu. A party of Franciscans
accompanied the Singhalese ambassadors to Ceylon,
where licence was given them to preach throughout the island. On this being known, Maaya Dunnai,
who by the death of his brother had succeeded to the
government of Raygam also, once more took up arms.
The king of Kotta was however accidentally shot by a
Portuguese gentleman, while at a party of pleasure on
the Kalaniganga; his death was regarded by his people
as a judgment on him for having sacrificed his country
and its interests to the foreigners. On his death, his son
Don Juan nominally embracing Christianity along with
a number of his followers, was raised to the throne.
Fresh wars followed, in which the Portuguese took a
leading part, rendering themselves by their rapacity, ty-

ranny, and cruelty, as great a scourge to friend as to foe.
In these wars the name of Maaya Dunnai is ever prominent, and his son, a mere lad, on his first expedition with
his father, displayed such intrepidity as to obtain the
by-name of Raja Singha, or the " Lion king." In these
engagements the foreigners were not always successful
and on more than one occasion we read of their churches
and settlements on the coast having been destroyed,
and their converts massacred.   During an attack on
Kotta A. D. 1563, such was the closeness of the seige,
that the Portuguese commander caused the flesh of the
slain to be salted lest provisions should fail ; and being
convinced that the place could never be maintained ef-
fectually as a fortress, he caused it to be dismantled,
and induced the king to take shelter at Colombo, where
he was both the tool and the victim of his nominal protectors. The Portuguese now sought to excite the apprehensions of the minor chiefs of the interior, at the increasing
power of Maaya Dunnai, urging them to embrace Christianity and form an alliance with themselves. So early as
1547, Jayaweira, the reigning king of Kandy, had intima-
ted his wish to adopt the Roman Catholic faith, and at his
request 120 men were sent towards Kandy from Batticalon
to protect him from the effects of the indignation of his
subjects ; but ere they reached their destination, the king.
who had already changed his mind, caused them to be
waylaid and slain. In 1550, his successor to the Kandian
throne made a similar request ; and in spite of the warning
they had already had, a second force was dispatched by
the Portuguese, which was attacked when within three
miles of Kandy, defeated, and forced to retire with a loss
of 700 men, half of whom were Europeans.

On the death of Maaya Dunnai in 1571, his son Raja Singha succeeded him. He contrived to reduce most of the minor princes to obedience, and made himself master of Kandy, the king escaping to Manaar, where he and his daughter were baptised, the king by the name of Don Philip, the princess by that of Donna Catherina; her name will appear again in the course of this history.

As soon as Raja Singha's arrangements were completed, he invested Colombo with a formidable force; but the Portuguese remained masters of the sea, and sent naval armaments to destroy and ravage the cities on the coasts. They even proceeded so far as the extreme south of the island, where they pillaged the magnificent temple of Dondera, and returned laden with spoil, after having inflicted indescribable sufferings on the wretched and innocent victims of their wrath. Discouraged by these disasters, by the intelligence that fresh re-inforcements were arriving to the aid of his enemies, and that his own subjects were in revolt, the grim old lion king raised the seige and retired to Setawakka. There he was roused from his lair by a formidable revolt of the Kandians, who, instigated by the Portuguese, and commanded by a Singhalese prince of Peredinia, who had been baptized by the name of Don Juan, poured down upon the dominions of Raja Singha and laid them waste " to the walls of his palace." But Don Juan, intoxicated by success, and indignant at the Portuguese for proposing to bestow the hand of Donna Catherina on another than himself, turned against his allies, drove them from Kandy, poisoned his rival, and once more marched against Raja Singha, whom he defeated near Kaduganava pass.

The old chief, the hero of a hundred fights, unable to endure these disasters, refused surgical aid and retired to his den at Setawakka, where he died at an advanced age, A. D. 1592.

Don Juan now ascended the throne by the name of Wimala Dharma. The delada relic had in 1560 been carried off to Goa and there publicly destroyed, by the arch-bishop, who with his own hand, in the presence of the viceroy and his court and in spite of the offer of a fabulous price for its possession by the king of Pegu, reduced it to powder in a mortar and then burnt it in a brazier of charcoal, after which the ashes were cast into the river.

Though there can be no reasonable doubt that the delada relic was thus destroyed, Don Juan succeeded in inducing the priests to believe that it had been preserved, and he produced an imitation of it which is at the present day enshrined at Kandy, and revered as genuine.

Don Philip having died at Manaar, his daughter Donna Catherina, a ward of the Portuguese, became the lawful successor to the throne. Her guardians sent an army to repel the usurper, and an engagement ensued in which they were at first successful; but Wimala Dharma returning to the charge routed the Portuguese, carried off and married the queen, and for twenty years reigned over the Kandian country.

Resolved however to chastise him, Jerome Azevedo was sent by the Portuguese to take the command in Ceylon, a captain, of whom a countryman has recorded the belief that his subsequent misfortunes,—(he died in prison at Lisbon,) were a judgment on him for his cruel!

ties to the Singhalese. He was known to compel mothers to caste their infants between mill-stones, previous to their own execution. At Galle he caused his soldiers to take up children on the points of their spears, that they might hear how the young cocks *(Gallas)* crowed. "He caused many men to be cast off the bridge at Mal-wane, for the troops to see the crocodiles devour them, and these creatures grew so used to the food, that at a whistle they would lift their heads above the water."*

And now succeeded a series of conflicts attended with varied success; the Singhalese maddened by their suffer-ings and the atrocities of their enemies, for once made common cause against them; the Portuguese troops be-came mutinous; and the interference of the viceroy of Goa was necessary to preserve the settlements in Cey-lon from ruin. At this period, A. D. 1597, died at Col-ombo, Don Juan Dharmapola, the nominal, and last legitimate king of Ceylon, bequeathing to the Portuguese by will that which he had never virtually possessed,— the sovereignty of the island.

Those chiefs who were not under the authority of Kandy or Jaffna now took the oaths of allegiance to their new masters, on the understanding that their cus-toms and religion should be ensured to them, while the ministers of Christianity should be free to exercise un-molested the influences of persuasion. A proposal was made to introduce the Portuguese laws, but was respect-fully declined and abandoned.

Thus all the maritime provinces, save Jaffna, passed over to the Portuguese, A. D. 1597. But from their

---

* Faria y Souza as quoted by Sir E. Tennent.

mountain fastnesses the hardy Kandians so keenly har-
assed the interlopers, that they were compelled to maintain an army of 20,000 men of whom 1,000 were Europeans; and the possession of their newly acquired dominion proved a burden, rather than that source of bound-
less wealth they had pictured to themselves, when the
cinnamon trade first allured them to seek its acquisition.

We shall now go back a little, and briefly trace the history of Jaffna, to its final subjugation by the Portuguese.
In 1544, Francis Xavier, a Roman Catholic Missionary
commonly called the apostle of the east by those of
his own persuasion, preached at Manaar with such success that numbers embraced Christianity. The Raja of
Jaffna incensed at their apostacy from their own religion,
caused 600 of the converts to be impaled. But as
usual with persecution, the faith he sought to destroy
only became more widely spread. His sons embracing
it, the eldest was executed, and the second escaped to
Goa. The Portuguese had shortly previous to this, visited the peninsula with an armed force, and extorted the
promise of an annual tribute from the Raja. They now
resolved to reduce him to obedience, though several
years elapsed before they executed their purpose. In
1518, Xavier visited the Jaffna Court, where he met with
a flattering reception, the king professing his willing-
ness to embrace Christianity, though it does not appear
that he ever did so. In 1560, an expedition was fitted
out at Goa by the Portuguese, which sailed for Jaffna
accompanied by the viceroy and the arch-bishop; and
after a solemn service on the shore conducted by the
latter, the army advanced to the assault of the northern
capital, which after a severe conflict, was taken, until the

king compelled to purchase the retention of his crown by the payment of a very heavy ransom and the surrender of Manaar to the conquerors. It was here that the sacred tooth, the destruction of which has already been described, and which had been entrusted to the Raja of Jaffna during the commotions in the Singhalese country, was taken by the Portuguese. In 1591, and 1604 respectively, expeditions were sent against Jaffna to punish its king for aid rendered to the Singhalese ; but on each occasion he succeeded in buying off his antagonists. In 1617, probably in consequence of some further acts of hostility, his capital was taken under " circumstances of singular barbarity ;" the king carried to Goa and there executed, his heir induced to enter a convent, and the peninsula formally incorporated with the Portuguese possessions in the island.

The Dutch.

The revolt of seven of the Dutch provinces from the oppressive yoke of Philip 2d of Spain, and their declaration of independence under the name of the Netherlands, are events which though properly belonging to European history, were not without their influence on affairs in the East : the newly formed states rapidly extending their commerce, ere long sought the Indian seas. In 1602 one of their vessels, commanded by admiral Spillbergen, anchored at Batticaloa, and the admiral was after some delay conducted to Kandy, where Wimala Dharma, who it will be remembered carried off and married Donna Catherina after defeating the Portuguese, was then reigning. On being satisfied that the strangers were not only unconnected with, but the enemies of the

Portuguese, the king in a transport of joy embraced the admiral, and in the fulness of his heart offered him permission to build a fort in the name of his master the Prince of Orange, in whatever part of the island he might select. Laden with gifts, the Dutch commander returned to Batticaloa, leaving his secretary and two musicians at the Kandian court; and having captured a Portuguese vessel off Batticaloa, he presented it with its crew and cargo to the king, as a pledge of his sincerity.

On the 27th April 1603, Sebald de Weert, the Dutch vice admiral, arrived at Batticaloa, and proceeding to the Kandian capital was received with every mark of regard and favor by Wimala Dharma. A treaty was entered into, whereby the Dutch commander pledged himself to aid the king against the Portuguese, and de Weert proceeded to Achin for the purpose of procuring reinforcements for his fleet, taking with him an ambassador from the Kandian court. On his return de Weert encountered and captured four Portuguese ships; and on his arrival at Batticaloa the king proceeded in person to meet him there, expecting to share in the prizes in terms of the treaty. He found however to his great mortification that de Weert had released the captured vessels; and his suspicions as to the good faith of the Dutch were further incited, by the representations of his ambassador, who complained that de Weert had at an entertainment treated him with marked disrespect by placing him at the foot of the table, though the representative of the king; while the Portuguese were seated at the head, from whence he inferred that their hostility was feigned. The ambassador further cautioned the king not to place himself within the power of the vice admiral, as he suspected him of treach-

taining treacherous designs. In consequence of those
representations, Wimala Dharma declined visiting the
Dutch fleet, or even entering a handsome tent which de
Weert had caused to be erected on the shore for his
reception.

Piqued at this mark of mistrust, de Weert abruptly
told the king that as he had thus slighted the attentions
paid him, he would not proceed to attack Galle, according to previous agreement, or render him any assistance.
On this an altercation ensued, during which de Weert,
who, to use the expression of the Dutch historian Baldæus "had drunk once more than was proper,"* made
use of some coarse and insulting expressions about the
Kandian queen. Fired with indignation, Wimala Dharma
ordered the Dutch commander to be seized. The
order was misunderstood, and de Weert was after some
resistance dispatched by the followers of the king. Having thus compromised himself, and perceiving that all
hope of conciliating the Dutch was at an end, Wimala
Dharma directed that the attendants of de Weert should
be likewise killed, with the exception of a youth whom
he took under his protection. A few escaped by
swimming to the ships: the rest were massacred. The
king then returned to Kandy, whence he dispatched
the following brief epistle to the Dutch officer the
next in command." " Que bebem vinho, nao he
bom. Deos ha faze justicia. Se quesieres pas, pas; se
guerra, guerra." " Who drinks wine is of no good. God
will do justice, if you desire peace, peace; if war, war."
- Wimala Dharma died not long after, of an excruciating

---

* "Sol had een meer als behoort gedronken hebbende."

7

ly painful disease, and Donna Catherina held the reins
of government alone. But her position was a painful
and difficult one. The prince of Uva, the most powerful
of the Kandian nobles, aspired to the throne, and as a
step towards gaining it, claimed the guardianship of the
late king's minor children. This claim was however
disputed by their uncle Senerat, a Budhist priest, who
contrived to murder his rival by stabbing him in the
back within the precincts of the royal palace, as both
were on their way to have an audience with the queen.
In justice to the murderer it should be added that he only
forestalled his victim in a similar design against his own
life. He succeeded in persuading the queen that his real
motive was regard for her safety and that of her children, and in inducing her to bestow her hand upon, and
share her throne with him, A. D. 1604.

Such was the desire of the Dutch to conciliate the
Singhalese, that they took no steps to avenge the slaugh-
ter of their countrymen. In 1609, a treaty offensive
and defensive was drawn up between the two powers.
The right to a monopoly of the trade in cinnamon,
gems, and pearls, was granted them ; they were permitted to build a fort at Kottiar near Trincomalie ; and
Marcellus de Boschhouwer, the Dutch—ambassador, was
detained at the Kandian court and treated with the most
marked distinction.

In 1612, a Portuguese force, conducted across the
island by an unfrequented route, surprised and destroyed the fort recently built by the Dutch at Kottiar, and
after putting the garrison to death, retired by way of the
Seven Korles. Here however they were overtaken
by a powerful force sent by the king of Kandy in

pursuit of them, which fell unexpectedly upon their rear, and at first put them to flight ; but rallying again, they turned on their assailants, and succeeded in defeating them and making themselves masters of the principality of Migone, which had been bestowed on the Dutch ambassador. On two subsequent occasions they advanced within a short distance of Kandy, and were repulsed with some difficulty. About this time Donna Catherina died, broken hearted at the loss of her eldest son, the heir apparent to the throne, whom Senerat was suspected of having poisoned. The king finding himself unable to make head against the Portuguese, dispatched Boschhouwer to the continent of India, in order to procure re-inforcements. Failing in his endeavors in that quarter, Boschhouwer proceeded to Holland ; but the states general, dissatisfied with his demeanor, and the position he assumed as an ambassador from a foreign court, rather than as a subject solicitous of advancing the interests of his own country, received him coldly, and refused their aid. Thereupon he proceeded to Copenhagen, and induced the Danes to send out a fleet to the help of the Kandian king. With this fleet Boschhouwer set sail, accompanied by his wife, and a military force levied for service in Ceylon. But Boschhouwer was not permitted to reach his destination ; he died on the voyage ; and on the arrival of the Danes in Ceylon, the king refused to ratify the treaty entered into with them by Boschhouwer.

In 1624, the Portuguese succeeded in inducing the king to enter into a treaty of amity with them ; but as they proceeded, in violation of it, to build a fort at Batticaloa, he resolved on attempting their destruction, without soliciting foreign aid. By means of his intrigues, the flames of revolt were kindled amongst the Singhalese subjects of the Portuguese, while the king held himself in readiness to turn to account the difficulties of his enemies. At length, in 1630, the Portuguese governor Don Constantine de Saa y Norona, misled by the insidious promises of some Kandian nobles, resolved to take the initiative, and to march, with all the forces he could collect, upon the province of Uva, the inhabitants of which, he was assured, were ready to rise in his favor. He was allowed to advance unmolested into the heart of that district, and to plunder and burn the town of Badulla: but on his return, the bulk of his Singhalese auxiliaries deserted him in a body at a given point, in conformity with an arrangement previously made between them and the enemy. Only 150 of them remained faithful; the Portuguese were surrounded on every side, and though they fought with the courage of despair, and succeeded in maintaining the unequal conflict till night, the torrents of rain which fell, prevented repose, damaged their ammunition, and rendered their arms unserviceable. Conscious of their approaching fate, the Portuguese troops entreated their commander to save himself under cover of the darkness; but this he nobly refused to do. The following morning witnessed his destruction, and that of his little band. His head was severed from his body and conveyed on a drum to the king, who was at the time bathing in the neighborhood. A. D. 1630.

The Kandians followed up this victory by a march on Colombo, which, but for the arrival of reinforcements from Goa, would in all probability have been taken, but thus strengthened, the besieged became the assailants; the king was defeated in the open field, and even compelled to purchase safety by the promise of paying an annual tribute of two elephants to the Portuguese.

In 1632 king Senerat died, and was succeeded by his son Raja Singha 2d. The Portuguese availing themselves of the occasion of the king's death to make an inroad on the Kandian dominions, Raja Singha sought a renewal of friendly intercourse with the Dutch. His overtures were joyfully accepted, and in January 1638, the Dutch admiral, Adam Westerwold, after defeating a Portuguese fleet in the neighborhood of Goa, dispatched two vessels, the Texel and the Dolphin, to Ceylon, in command of the commodore Koster, with directions to prepare the king for his own arrival, with the rest of the fleet, in the month of May following.

Apprised of this new alliance, the Portuguese determined to attack Kandy before the rest of the Dutch force arrived. The king retired from the city, which the Portuguese sacked and burnt; but on their return, they were attacked by an overwhelming force; their native troops deserted them; their overtures were rejected, and their commanders, Diego de Melo, and Damijao Bottado, with the whole Portuguese force, except seventy who were made prisoners, perished on the field of battle.

On the first of May 1638, Westerwold arrived with the rest of the Dutch fleet, and at once attacked and took the Portuguese fort at Batticaloa. The following year he took the fort at Trincomalie, which, as well as that at Batticaloa, he entirely destroyed, in compliance with the wishes of the king. Negombo, Matura, and Galle, fell in succession; and the king of Kandy invested Colombo, which he might, if so disposed, have taken : but unwilling that the Dutch should overcome all opposition, and desirous rather of playing off the one European power against the other, he raised the seige, and even afforded the Portuguese an opportunity of recovering Negombo. Prior to raising the seige of Colombo, the commodore Koster, who, unmindful of the fate of de Weert, had assumed a haughty and offensive bearing at the Kandian court, was murdered on his way from the capital to Batticaloa, by some subjects of the king. In 1646, an armistice was concluded between Portugal and the Netherlands, one of the articles of agreement being that each power should retain without molestation from the other, whatever possessions it had already acquired in Ceylon.

The king of Kandy however, by this time as much dissatisfied with the Dutch as with the Portuguese, used every means in his power to embroil them with each other, and himself attacked the possessions of either, whenever an opportunity offered itself. On one occasion he boldly marched through the Portuguese territory to Negombo, where he attacked the Dutch in their fort, which he succeeded in taking; and having made prisoners of the garrison, he wrapped in silk cloths the heads of such officers as had fallen in the conflict, and dispatched them to the Dutch commander at Galle. To this insult, as well as to many others heaped on them, the Dutch either submitted in silence, or sought to conciliate their haughty enemies by the most abject marks of humiliation. Their great object was gain, and for that, they were content to waive for the present, every other consideration. They were wont to forward periodically

to the Kandian court, such offerings as they believed
would be most acceptable; and these were accompanied
with messages of profound respect and submission. At
times their presents were refused, and their messengers
maltreated, and dismissed with disgrace; at other times
demands were made of them by the king for such gifts
as he was desirous of receiving, in terms which implied
that it was their privilege no less than their duty to
minister to his inclinations. They succeeded by their arts
in retaining the fort of Galle, and in recovering that of
Negombo, as well as the prisoners which had been taken
at the seige of the latter. These forts were highly
prized, because situated on the confines of the cinnamon plantations, on which the Dutch set so great a
value.

The armistice between the Dutch and the Portuguese
having expired A. D. 1650, the former attacked and
made themselves masters of Caltura, with the aid of the
Kandians, who saw fit once more to unite themselves
with the Dutch. Colombo was next assailed; and after
having been reduced by famine to such extremities
that two mothers are said to have eaten their own children, capitulated, A. D. 1656.* No sooner however had
victory crowned their efforts, than the allied besiegers
quarrelled about the partition of their prizes; and an engagement ensued between themselves, in which the
Kandians were worsted; on which Raja Singha entered
into a treaty of friendship with his former enemies, the
Portuguese. In 1658, the Dutch attacked and took from
the Portuguese the forts of Manaar and Jaffna; and be-

* Baldæus, Chapter 35, Dutch Edition.

came masters of all the sea board of the island. Raja Singha returned to his own capital, where his oppression and cruelty became so intolerable to his subjects that they revolted, and on his seeking safety by flight, they proclaimed his son, a mere child, his successor: but the boy, unwilling to accept the intended honor, found means to escape to his father; and the rebels becoming disheartened, the king ventured to return to Kandy, succeeded in quelling the rebellion, and cruelly chastised those who had caused his flight. Fearing that his son might hereafter prove refractory, the unnatural parent caused him to be put to death. Whilst these disturbances continued in the interior, the Dutch enjoyed some respite, of which they availed themselves to strengthen their position on the sea coast; after which, feeling more secure against attack, they were enabled to carry on, though entirely on behalf of their government, a brisk trade with Europe, as well as with the neighboring countries in the east.

It will be no matter of wonder in these days of free trade, to learn that notwithstanding a most rigid monopoly of the trade in cinnamon, elephants, arecanuts, sapanwood, chaya-roots, pepper, cardamums, &c.; and in spite of heavy taxes on lands, iron ore, jaggery, fish, &c, their possessions in the island were a source of annual loss to the Dutch. Baron van Imhoff, one of their governors, compares Ceylon to those costly tulips of Holland, which, intrinsically worth but little, bore a fabulous value. Peculation was universal amongst all classes of the public service; so much so, that although the salary of a governor was, exclusive of rations and allowances, only £30 per month, two or three years' tenure of office secured ample wealth to the occupant; and the public accounts were totally unreliable, being intentionally and systematically falsified. At length, in 1726, the governor, Petrus Vuyst, conceived the idea of throwing off his allegiance to the Netherlands, and rendering himself an independent sovereign. His designs were however discovered, and he was carried to Batavia, where his body, after having been broken on the wheel, was burnt, and his ashes thrown into the sea. He was succeeded by Stephanus Versluys, an extortionate and cruel tyrant.

War having broken out between Louis the 14th of France, and the Netherlands, A. D. 1672, a French fleet took possession of Trincomalie; and the Dutch thereupon hastily evacuated the forts of Kottiar and Batticaloa; the French departed however, shortly after, being unable to maintain their position in the island, and the Dutch re-occupied the places they had lost. On their arrival, the French had sent an embassy to the king of Kandy, who hailed their advent, with great joy, hoping they would aid him against the Dutch, as the Dutch had aided his predecessor, against the Portuguese: but their ambassador, unacquainted with, or indifferent to the haughty character of the king, violated the rules of etiquette laid down at his court, by passing the royal palace on horseback, on his first arrival in Kandy. He subsequently testified his annoyance at being detained some time before being admitted to an audience, by abruptly quitting the precincts of the palace, and drawing his sword on some of the officers of the king who attempted to stop him. For this indignity the king caused the ambassador and his suite to be flogged and put in chains, with the exception of two envoys who had preceeded him. The ambassador was kept thus imprisoned for six months; though his companions were soon released from confinement, on satisfying the king that they were not active parties to the affront offered him. They were however all detained in the Kandian country, as prisoners.

Raja Singha 2d, died in 1687. His two successors, in turn maintained peace with the Dutch, who on their part materially assisted them in obtaining from Arracan a chapter of Budhist priests, the national religion having fallen into such decay as to render this measure necessary.

The Singhalese royal race became extinct in the person of Koondesala, who died in 1739. A Tamulian, a brother of the Queen Dowager was accordingly raised to the throne with the title of Sri Wijayo Raja. It had long been customary for the kings of Ceylon to marry Tamil wives, thus preparing the way for a total transfer of the crown to that race, the blood of which already flowed so largely in the veins of the royal family: no Singhalese king ever again ascended the throne of Ceylon.

During Wijayo's reign, the Kandians prevailed on the low country Singhalese to attempt the expulsion of the Dutch. But the latter not only defeated their opponents, but marched on Kandy, which they took, and held for some time, the king having retired on their approach. In 1766, Governor Iman Willem Falck, a man of enlarged mind, who had already inaugurated a more enlightened policy within the dominions of the Dutch in the island, concluded an advantageous treaty with the Kandians, whereby a considerable extent of territory was secured to the Netherlands, and conditions favorable to the extension of trade between the coast and the interior were entered into. The results of the liberal policy of the. new governor soon became apparent in the improved condition of the trade and revenue of the Dutch possessions.

The British.

In 1782, war was declared between the Dutch and the English; and the latter, who had by this time established themselves at Calcutta, Madras, Bombay, and other places on the coast of India, directed their efforts against Trincomalie; and having taken possession of it, Mr. Hugh Boyd, a civil servant of the E. I. Company, was dispatched to Kandy as an ambassador. Communications of a friendly nature had been opened between the Madras government and the Kandian court so early as 1763; but the British had failed to avail themselves of the arrangements for an alliance then made, and in consequence of this slight, Mr. Boyd's overtures were rejected; and on his return to Trincomalie he had the further mortification of finding that during his absence the French had surprised the fort and carried off the English garrison. They restored the place to the Dutch, with whom they were on friendly terms, the following year.

In 1795, war broke out afresh between the Dutch and the Kandians, on which the latter solicited from the British that aid they had previously rejected. An armament was accordingly dispatched to their help from Madras, which took possession in rapid succession, of Trincomalie, Jaffna, Calpentyn, and Negombo. Colombo capitulated with scarce the show of resistance; and the Dutch possessions in the island, which had not yet fallen into the hands of the English, were ceded to them, including the fortresses of Galle, Caltura, and Matura ; their respective garrisons being allowed to vacate them with all the honors of war. The public buildings, records, and treasure, were made over to the victors, and the public servants and residents were allowed the option of remaining or leaving as they saw fit. Most of the judicial officers and clergymen chose to remain, retaining their appointments and emoluments as before.

Much has been said of the pusillanimity of the Dutch in thus surrendering all they held in the island, almost without striking a blow. But there is reason for suspecting that treachery on the part of their commander, not cowardice on that of their soldiers, was the real cause. It is known that previous to the advance of the British on Colombo by land after the taking of Negombo, an English officer landed from the fleet, which was at the time hovering off the coast, and after conferring with the Dutch governor, re-embarked. On his departure, some Swiss mercenaries in the service of the Dutch were allowed unmolested to transfer their allegiance to the English. Van Angelbeek then concealed his valuables, and calmly awaiting the advance of the attacking army, at once capitulated on its arrival : but such was the indignation of his troops at the surrender of Colombo, that they spat at, and attempted to strike the British as they marched into the fort, and nothing but the presence of the English saved Van Angelbeek from the effects of the resentment of his own countrymen : he never revisited the land of his birth, but remained a resident in the island until his death, which is said by some to have been caused by his own hand. Thus ended the rule of the

Dutch in Ceylon; a rule, which though marked by fewer atrocities than that of the Portuguese, had also its dark spots. The object of the Dutch, though better concealed, was in reality the same; they aimed at the entire subjugation of the island; and wherever they succeeded in fixing their yoke, its wearers found it a heavy one.

The maritime districts of the island having been thus transferred to the British, they were placed under the government of Madras, and Mr. Andrews, a civil servant of that presidency, who had previously been appointed ambassador to the Kandian court, was entrusted with the adjustment of the financial system to be pursued in the newly acquired possessions.

The course adopted by him was unfortunate. Regardless of local differences, he introduced into the island that system which prevailed in Madras, swept away the one previously existing, and instead of employing the native officials and headmen of the island to carry out the scheme, supplied their places by rapacious dubashes from India, intent on extortion and oppression. The dissatisfaction caused by these measures led to a revolt. It was soon suppressed, but the necessity for pursuing a different course from that prevalent in India, became apparent to the home government; the Hon. Frederick North, subsequently Earl of Guildford, was in 1798, appointed governor; and in 1802, when by the treaty of Amiens the Dutch possessions in Ceylon were formally transferred to the British, all connection with Madras was severed; an arrangement to which Ceylon in a great measure owes her subsequent prosperity.

Two years after the occupation of the maritime

provinces by the British, Rajadhi Raja Singha, the king of Kandy, died A. D. 1798, leaving no issue. It devolved therefore on the adigar, or prime minister, according to the laws and usages of the country, to nominate his successor.

Pileme Talawe, who at this time held that office, an ambitious, designing, and unscrupulous man, now conceived the idea of overthrowing the Tamil dynasty, and placing himself upon the throne. With this end in view, he selected for the crown, a brother of the queen, a Tamulian youth about eighteen years of age ; who was accordingly crowned with the title of Wikreme Raja Singha: he was the last king of Kandy.

The adigar next turned his eyes towards the British, with the hope of enlisting their services in his favor. He opened communications with the Governor, Mr. North, who did not consider it unworthy of the English name, to countenance the designs of the traitor, and even to promise him his assistance.

It was accordingly arranged between them that an embassy should be sent to Kandy, and that the ambassador to be selected should be the principal military officer in the island ; that his escort should in reality consist of a strong military force, well provided with cannon and munition of war; that when the plan was ripe for execution, the king should on some pretence or other be deposed and conveyed to Jaffna, that the adigar should be raised to the throne, nominally recognised as king, and supported in his position by a British force, to be paid out of the Kandian treasury.

Accordingly general Mac Dowall proceeded towards Kandy with a powerful and well appointed " escort" of artillery and infantry. But the suspicions of the king regarding the real character of the " embassy" were aroused by some of his officers. The king accordingly caused the party to be guided by a circuitous route, which was impassable for cannon ; and the ambassador was consequently obliged to leave them, as well as the greater part of his force, at Ruanwelle, and to proceed to Kandy, with a diminished party ; and after having been delayed for some time on various pretences, the proposals for a treaty made by him were rejected, and he was obliged to return to Colombo without having accomplished his purpose.

But the quiver of the treacherous adigar contained more arrows than one. He stirred up the mind of the king against the British, and induced him to molest their borders and their subjects, with a view to embroil him with the English, and so to afford them a pretext for war. A party of traders who proceeded to the interior, having been robbed and ill treated, compensation was demanded by the British government, and refused. Upon this General Mac Dowall advanced on Kandy with a force of 3.000 men, (A. D. 1803.) On his approach, the king retired to Hanguranketty, after having fired the town. By the secret suggestions of the adigar, who still kept up communication with the invaders, one Muttuswamy, a relative of the king, a man of no moral character, and despised by the people, was placed on the throne ; and he was induced to agree to the proposal that a British force should remain to support him on the throne, and that a valuable tract of territory should be ceded to his protectors, as a reward for their services.

The adigar next proposed,—and the proposal was list-

ened to, that the newly crowned king should be deposed, that the fugitive king should be given up to the
English; and that the adigar himself should be raised
to the chief authority under them, with the title of " chief
prince." The general, after promising his consent to these
contemplated measures, quitted Kandy on the 1st April
1803, leaving behind him 300 European and 700 Malay
soldiers, as the British contingent. The numbers of those
who remained, were however soon thinned by sickness
to such an extent as materially to weaken the efficiency
of the force; and the adigar, false to the foreigners, as
he had been to his own king, and mindful only of himself, now formed the daring plan of making himself
master of the person of Mr. North, destroying the contingent in Kandy, murdering both kings, and assuming
the crown himself. The opportunity of which he hoped
to avail himself for effecting the first of his designs, was
at an interview agreed on between himself and the governor, in the Seven Korles. The meeting took place, but
his purpose was frustrated by the opportune, and hu-
manly speaking, accidental arrival of a detachment of
Malays which at the time happened to be on the march.

Foiled in this, he resolved to attempt the second of
his designs. On the 24th June, the palace in Kandy, in
which the British troops were quartered, was attacked
by a strong body of Kandians. At this time there were
but twenty Europeans fit for duty, so much had sickness
reduced their numbers. Accordingly, after an attempt
at resistance, Major Davie, the officer in command, was
induced to listen to a proposal that he should evacuate
the town, in favor of the deposed king; that he should
take with him the puppet Muttuswamy; that he should

be allowed to retire unmolested to Colombo, with arms
and baggage; that facilites should be afforded for his
progress thither; and that the sick should remain in the
hospitals and be tended and carefully watched. The
terms of the capitulation having been signed by the adigar on behalf of the king, Major Davie marched out of
the town the same evening, with fourteen European officers, 20 European soldiers, 250 Malays, and the ex
king Muttuswamy. At a distance of about three miles
from the town they reached the banks of the Mahawille
ganga, which, swollen by the floods, rolled turbulently
by, and forbad passage save by boats. No arrangements
appeared however to have been made for their crossing,
and they were consequently compelled to halt until the
following day, in this unfavorable situation.

The morning came, but no boats or rafts appeared;
the Kandians began to assemble around them in force,
and at length a message was brought to the effect that
the king was much enraged at Muttuswamy's having
been permitted to accompany them, and that it would
be necessary to give him up immediately. This, Major
Davie refused to do; on which a second message, more
peremptory than the first, was sent to him, with promises
of aid in the event of compliance, and threats of vengeance in case of refusal. After a consultation with the
other officers, Major Davie consented to give him up;
he was carried back to Kandy and there executed along
with two of his relations. Several of his followers were
cruelly mutilated, and a few of them subsequently
escaped to the sea coast and were provided for by the
British government.

The tragedy now draws towards its close. After a de-

tention of two days on the banks of the river, the British
troops were ordered to lay down their arms and return
to Kandy, with the assurance that their lives would be
spared. They complied with the first part of the order.
The English were then led away two at a time, and
when out of sight of their comrades, ruthlessly butchered, and their bodies thrown into a hollow. Major Davie and Captain Rumley were the only ones intentionally
spared; they were taken back to Kandy, and ended their
days in captivity, though allowed a certain amount of
liberty. During the massacre, an officer of the Bengal
artillery, Captain Humphreys by name, and a medical
assistant, a native of Colombo, contrived to throw themselves amongst the slain as if dead, and when darkness
set in, concealed themselves as they best could. The
medical assistant escaped to Colombo; the officer was
eventually made prisoner and detained in Kandy for
the rest of his life. A corporal, called Barnsley, was
wounded and left for dead, but he recovered and made
his way to Fort Mac Dowall, where a detachment of the
British was stationed.

Before passing judgment on the officer who commanded this ill-fated party, it should be remembered that he
never had the opportunity afforded him of vindicating
himself. It should also be remembered that it was at
the urgent entreaty of his brother officers that the
capitulation was agreed to by him; that it was after
consultation with them that he surrendered the unhappy
Muttuswamy, and then only, when refusal appeared
useless; and that it was with the concurrence of the
majority that the fatal step was taken of laying down
their arms. During the late Indian mutiny, instances

of misplaced confidence, as striking, are on record, where
the parties principally concerned were men of known
and acknowledged bravery. Let us endeavor to realize the
effects of sickness, hunger, and fatigue, upon the strongest
constitutions ; the influences of physical debility on the
mind ; the hopeless position of.the party, with a swollen ·
river before them, a hostile city behind them, and a powerful force around them,—and we shall be the better able
to understand how they were induced to give ear to the
blandishments of a heartless and deceitful villain, who
had hitherto pretended to be their friend, and who spoke
of repose to the weary, and safety to the imperilled. It
would have been well, as the event proved, to have tried
to hold their ground within the city until reinforcements
could be obtained : it would have been better, when they
found themselves betrayed, to have died where they
stood, with arms in their hands : but it is easy to be wise
after the act. They were British officers and British
soldiers, and with such, bravery is the rule not the exception ; doubtless under more favorable circumstances
they would have shewn themselves worthy of their country and their service. Those who believe that a super-
intending providence guides the affairs of men, and
sometimes allows them to suffer, in this world, the punishment of national sins, will perhaps regard this temporary humiliation of the British arms as a chastisement
from above : for we cannot disguise from ourselves the
fact that it was not creditable to those concerned therein,
to connive at the villany of the adigar, whatever might
be the ulteror objects to be gained by so doing.

On the arrival of Corporal Barnsley with the sad
intelligence, at Fort Mac Dowall, eighteen miles east of

Kandy, Captain Madge, the officer in command, abandoned the position, and though obliged to leave most of the
sick behind him, succeeded in fighting his way to Trincomalie : he was much molested during the first part of
his retreat, but falling in, happily, with a party on the
march to Kandy, the detachments united, and made
their way to Trincomalie without further hindrance.
Another officer, ensign Grant, who was posted in a mis-
erable redoubt at Dambedinia, held his position with a
handful of Europeans and Malays, resisting alike the
attacks and the insidious overtures of the Kandians. He
was reinforced, and subsequently relieved ; and the
party marched into Colombo with scarce the loss of a man.

After the massacre of the Europeans of Major Davie's
party, the Malays attached to it were offered their lives,
if they would take service under the Kandian king.
Under the circumstances it is scarcely to be wondered
at that most of them accepted the conditions : there were
however two exceptions, and their fidelity is worthy of
the highest honor.   Captain Nouradeen and his brother
refused to be false to their colors, and professed themselves ready to suffer death in preference.   They were
carried back to Kandy, where the king himself renewed
the offer, with the promise of honorable employment ;
but they persisted in their noble resolve, in spite of the
fate which they knew awaited them ; and the ignoble tyrant ordered them to be executed, after which their
bodies, denied the rites of burial, were thrown into the
jungle.   Many of the private soldiers found means to
escape from their forced service in Kandy, and to
join their comrades in Colombo.   The sick Europeans,
120 in number, who had been left in the hospitals in

Kandy, had been butchered in cold blood, shortly after the capitulation.

Deep as was the consternation felt at Colombo on the receipt of the sad intelligence, much time was not left the British for lamentation. The king of Kandy, believing the tide of fortune to have turned in his favor, resolved to pour down his forces in overwhelming numbers from the hills. He accordingly attacked the British in every quarter simultaneously, while at the same time he succeeded in kindling the flames of revolt amongst their Singhalese dependents throughout the whole island. He in person led the attack upon the fort at Hangwelle, about 18 miles from Colombo: and so certain did he feel of victory, that his followers brought with them the instruments of torture which he had prepared for the prisoners he expected to make. But instead of victory he met with signal defeat; he was forced to retreat precipitately, and several of the guns and muskets which he had taken from Major Davie, were here recaptured.

The British were however not in a position to carry the war at once into the heart of the enemy's country. In 1804, preparations were made for an invasion, but the design was for the time abandoned. There is however an episode connected with the intended movement, which did much to restore the prestige of the British name. Captain Johnstone had been ordered to march on Kandy from Batticaloa, and there to join the force it was intended to concentrate at that city. By some oversight, this order was not countermanded, when the scheme was abandoned, and he accordingly penetrated to the mountain capital, with a party of 300 men, of whom only 82 were

Europeans, and there held his ground for three days, when, finding himself unsupported, he fought his way to Trincomalie, with the loss of only ten killed, and with six wounded. Ambuscades lined the whole road ; and his escape from complete destruction was attributed by the astonished natives to supernatural agency.

The position of the British for the two following years was one of inaction. A renewal of the war with France prevented reinforcements being sent to Ceylon, and the operations of their troops were confined to punishing those of their subjects who had revolted. Opportunities for soliciting a pardon were afforded the king of Kandy, but he refused to avail himself of them, and threw the blame of the massacre near Kandy on the adigar. In spite of all that had occurred, this subtle traitor contrived to hold his office for some time longer, probably because too powerful to be treated as a foe. At length he was fairly detected in a conspiracy against the king's life, (1812.) He was thereupon sentenced to be beheaded, and his nephew Eheylepola was raised to his vacant post.

Whatever may be thought of the part Mr. North took with regard to the political affairs of the interior, it must be said that during his administration, the well-being of Her Majesty's subjects in the maritime district was greatly promoted. Religion, education, and commerce were encouraged, the administration of justice placed on an improved footing, and agriculture extended. Mr. North was succeeded by Sir Thomas Maitland, (1805,) who was in turn followed by General Wilson, as Lieutenant Governor, (1811,) and he again by General Brownrigg, (1812.) Under these governors the resources of the island were further developed, and protection afforded to all classes alike.

It was not however until 1815, twelve years after the outrage previously related, that retribution visited the Kandian king. That blood thirsty tyrant pursued the victims of his suspicions or displeasure, with a cruelty absolutely fiendish; he employed the labor of his subjects on works of little utility, and punished arbitrarily, those who ventured to remonstrate with him. Eheylepola, the new adigar, appears to have inherited much of the ambition and spirit of intrigue of his predecessor; and his acts having aroused the suspicions of the king, he was directed to proceed to the district of Saffragam, over which he held the office of dissave.

The king's mistrust of the adigar having been strengthened by charges preferred against him after his departure from Kandy, an order was sent recalling him forthwith; conscious of the fate that awaited him if he returned, the adigar refused to obey the summons, excited the people of Saffragam to revolt, and solicited the aid of the British. But his schemes being discovered, he was formally deposed from the office of adigar, and Molligodde dissave, who was appointed in his stead, was ordered to march on Saffragam, and quell the revolt. On his approach, the rebels were seized with a panic, and Eheylepola finding resistance hopeless, fled to Colombo, and placed himself under the protection of the governor. Disappointed of his prey, the king resolved to wreak his vengeance on the innocent relations of the offender; for he had unfortunately left them in Kandy. The sentence pronounced against them was, that the wife and children of Eheylepola, his brother

and his brother's wife, should be put to death. His wife
and children were accordingly brought forth from prison,
and placed between the Nata and Maha Vishnu De'wa'les.
The mother then called upon her eldest son, a lad about
eleven years of age, to meet his death with fortitude ;
but the boy, terrified at the prospect, clung to his mother,
whereon his brother, who was two years younger, stop-
ped forward, and bade him not fear, for he would shew
him the way to die. Before the eyes of the mother, her
children were successively decapitated, and—horrible
to relate, she was compelled by the inhuman tyrant,
under the threat of the most disgraceful ill-treatment in
case of refusal, to pound their inanimate heads in a
mortar as they were successively severed by the exe-
cutioner. When the youngest, a babe in arms, had been
torn from the bosom, and an end in like manner
put to its brief existence, the mother, her sister-in-
law, and two other females were conveyed to the Bo-
gambera lake, and there drowned.

Accustomed as the Kandians were to scenes of torture,
this fresh manifestation of his cruelty produced a state of
feeling against the tyrant, impossible to describe. Sir
E. Tennent remarks that he has verified the account
on record by the testimony of persons still alive, " who
were spectators of a scene that after the lapse of forty
years is still spoken of with a shudder ;" and it is said that
for two days the whole city, with the exception of the
royal palace, was as one house of mourning, no fires
were lighted, and no food dressed. One dissave had
fainted at the sight of the executions, and this manifestation of feeling cost him his office.

But the family of Eheylapola were not the only vic-

tims of the tyrant's resentment; others followed; and
the chiefs and people, uncertain who would be the next
sufferer, looked around for deliverance, and turned their
eyes towards the British, to aid them in throwing off the
thraldom of their oppressor. Circumstances ere long
occurred which rendered the necessity for his chastisement imperative. In 1814, a party of native traders,
British subjects, proceeded to the interior; and the king,
suspecting them to be spies, caused their noses, ears, and
arms to be cut off. Those who survived the mutilation
returned to Colombo, and on the circumstances being
made known, war was declared by the British, (July 10th
1815,) with the announcement however, that it would
be waged " not against the Kandians' as a nation, but
against that tyrannical power which had provoked by
aggravated outrages and indignities the just resentment
of the British nation ; which had cut off the most ancient
and noble families in the kingdom, deluged the land with
the blood of its subjects, and by the violation of every
religious and moral law, become an object of abhorrence
to mankind." (Proclamation as quoted by Philalethes.)
The British forces were formed into eight divisions,
and were ordered to concentrate themselves upon the
Kandian capital, proceeding thither by different routes.
The division which advanced from Colombo, marched
by Ruanwelle, encountered, and defeated a large force
sent to oppose it, commanded by Molligodde in person,
who narrowly escaped capture by plunging into the
jungle, his palanquin falling into the hands of the victors. But although Molligodde had assumed an attitude
apparently hostile to the British, his sympathies were
with them; and so soon as his family had succeeded in

escaping from the reach of the king's resentment, he
openly threw up his allegiance, and went over to the
invaders, accompanied by most of the other chiefs. The
meeting between Eheylepola and Molligodde has been
described by Philalethes. The remembrance of their mutual sorrows excited the most painful feelings, and they
both burst into tears.

As the British force closed in upon the capital, the
king, who is described as having hitherto continued " in
a state of torpid inactivity," began to awaken to a
sense of the dangers that surrounded him, and to be conscious of the dissatisfaction of his subjects. The only effect however that it appeared to have on him was an increased desire of gratifying his vindictive spirit, and it
became dangerous in the extreme to communicate to
him any intelligence of a disastrous nature ; of two messengers who were charged with the news of a defeat,
he caused one to be beheaded, and the other to be impaled.

On the 14th February 1815, the British entered Kandy : the king and two of his wives had fled to Medema-
hanewera, whither he was pursued by a party of Eheylepola's retainers, commanded by a chief called Eknel-
ligodde.

The place of the king's concealment having been
pointed out to them, the door was shattered, when the
glare of torches revealed the tyrant to the gaze of his
exulting subjects, who " bound him hand and foot, re-
viled him, spat on him, and dragged him to the next village with every species of insult and indignity" (Philalethes.) Mean spirited in the hour of adversity, as he
had been arrogant in the day of power, he supplicated

at the hands of Eheylepola's retainers that mercy he had
refused their master's family.   His life was spared, but
he was conveyed a prisoner to Colombo, and thence removed to Vellore in the Madras presidency, where he
died A. D. 1832, of dropsy.

We extract the following interesting passage from Sir
Emerson Tennent's work. " On the 2d March 1815, a
solemn convention of the chiefs assembled in the audience hall of the palace of Kandy, at which a treaty was
concluded formally deposing the king and vesting his
dominions in the British crown ; on condition that the national religion should be maintained and protected, justice impartially administered to the people, and the chiefs
guarranteed in their ancient privileges and powers. Eheylepola, who had cherished the expectation that the crown
would have descended to his own head, bore the disap-
pointment with dignity, declined the offers of high office,
and retired with the declaration that his ambition was
satisfied by being recognized as the friend of the British
government."

The account of the forms observed on this occasion
may be thought interesting. The British governor was
seated at the upper end of the hall of audience, while the
troops were drawn up in the square before the palace.
Eheylepola was then ushered in by himself ; he was received with demonstrations of respect, and a seat assigned him at the governor's right hand. Molligodde
then advanced as first adigar, and introduced the principal dissaves and chiefs. Expressions of mutual regard
and esteem were exchanged, the governor thanking them
for the assistance they had rendered the troops when
marching through their respective districts, and the chiefs

on their part observing that they viewed the British as
protectors who had rescued the country from tyranny
and oppression. "The treaty was then read in English
by the deputy secretary, and afterwards in Singhalese by
the modeliar. The tall and venerable dissave of Godapola
expressed the full concurrence of the Kandian chiefs.
Molligodde and the other chiefs then proceeded to the
great door of the hall, where the korales, mohottales,
and other subordinate headmen from the different districts were attending with a great concourse of the inhabitants ; and the headmen having arranged themselves
according to their respective divisions, the treaty was
again read by the modeliar in Singhalese.   At the con-
clusion the British flag was hoisted, and a royal salute
from the cannon of the city announced His Majesty
George 3d, sovereign of the whole island of Ceylon,
March 2d 1815." * Thus was the British government inaugurated in the Kandian provinces, with the consent
of all the parties concerned.   But although the people
acquired a larger degree of freedom and protection than
they had ever before enjoyed, it was hardly to be expected that the chiefs, accustomed to almost unlimited
power over their vassals, would submit without dissatisfaction to the curtailment of their authority, or assimilate themselves at once with a form of government so
different from that to which they had been accustomed.
The instances, if there be any, are rare, where a people

* The account of this interering ceremony is taken from a
little compilation called the history of Ceylon, published by the
Singhalese tract society Kandy, 1858, a work which, had it not
been confined to the history of the island, would have rendered
the publication of this one unnecessary.

has not at first fretted under foreign rule; and the fact of that rule being one of their own selection, would scarcely mitigate the feeling of dissatisfaction. Before two years had elapsed, the smouldering embers of discontent had been fanned into the flame of rebellion. It first broke out amidst the lovely valleys of Uva; the principal officer of government in the district was killed by an arrow, while attempting to pacify the malcontents; the disturbance spread to the three and four Korles, Udenuwera, and Yattenuwera; and a pretender to the throne was pushed forward, whose standard every chief of importance joined, Kapitapola, the brother-in law of Eheylepola, being appointed his first adigar.

The dense forests, mountain passes, rivers, and ravines of the interior, afforded every facility to the insurgants, while they presented formidable obstacles to the British; and sickness, caused by exposure, likewise increased their difficulties. No other way of quelling the rebellion appeared feasible, than that of destroying the houses, property, and gardens in those districts where the inhabitants were up in arms; and painful as this course was to both parties, it was adopted. Reinforcements arrived ere long from India to the aid of the British, while on the contrary disaffection spread amongst the Kandians themselves; their councils were divided, and at length the quarrel rose so high between Madugalle, a chief of Dumbera, and Kapitapola, that the form. or out of revenge exposed to the public the real character of the pretender, (who, so far from being in any way connected with the royal family, was a man of obscure birth;) and put him in the stocks!

Thus terminated the rebellion of 1817. Ten thousand

of the inhabitants of the central province had died, either in action, by fever, or by famine, the whole population of the disaffected districts, men, women, and children, had been living in the cold forests ; their fields had lain uncultivated for two years, their fruit trees had been cut down, and their cattle and grain had been carried off or destroyed. The prime movers in the rebellion fell into the hands of the British, and were dealt with according to circumstances. Pileme Talawa, the son of the former adigar, and Kapitapola, were captured near Anuradha- pura, by an officer, well known in Ceylon at the present day, as general Fraser ; and Madugalle was soon after taken. Pileme Talawa, and Eheylepola, who had also taken part in the rebellion, were banished to the Mauri- tius, and the two others were executed in the island.

The British regarded this as a suitable opportunity for remodelling the judicial and revenue administration of the interior. It was evidently necessary that the al- most irresponsible power of the chiefs should be brought within bounds, and this was accordingly done. It was also necessary that some alteration should be made with regard to the relative positions of the government and the priesthood, many of whom had aided and influenced the rebels. By the proclamation of 1815 it had been provided "that the religion of Budha" should be "in- violate, and its rites and places of worship be main- tained and protected." After the rebellion it was provided by the proclamation of 1818, that "the priests as well as the ceremonies of the Budhist religion should receive the respect which in former times was shewn them," equal protection being at the same time given "to all religions." This proclamation, if not all that could be wished, was less opposed to the principles of Christianity than the former one, and relieved the government from much of the embarrassment that the other would, have occasioned had it continued in force.

Notwithstanding the severe lesson the Kandians had been taught in 1817—18, another pretender arose at Welasse, in 1820; in 1823, a Budhist priest created some disturbance at Matele ; in 1824, a plot of a treasonable character was discovered in Bintenne ; in 1830, several arrests for sedition were made ; in 1835, six chiefs were tried for treason ; in 1843, a priest was brought to justice for a similar offence, at Badulla; and in 1848, an extensive rising took place, in which the rebels suffered very severely.

In all these attempts to throw off the foreign yoke, the Kandians were doubtless encouraged by the recollection of their former successful resistance to the aggression of the Portuguese and Dutch. They forgot however, that the obstacles which their mountain passes, foaming torrents, and thorny gates once presented, existed no longer. No sooner had the rebellion of 1817 been quelled, than Sir Robert Brownrigg formed the resolution of penetrating, by a military road, to the very heart of the mountain region : it was however left for his successor to carry out, with all his characteristic vigor, the execution of this purpose. Sir Edward Barnes at once grasped the idea, and soon, over rivers, through rocks, and by declivities, a broad, well constructed road wound along the steep sides of the mountain zone, and terminated in the town of Kandy :—henceforth successful rebellion was at an end. The completion of this work was the signal for the commencement of others of a similar char-

acter, and at the present day, Ceylon may boldly submit
to a comparison with any other British colony in the
world, with regard to well constructed roads and handsome and substantial bridges.

We now approach a period in the history of Ceylon,
which may almost be said to belong to the present day ;
a mere outline will be given of the leading events that
have occurred since the time of Sir Edward Barnes, who
laid the foundation of that prosperity to which the island
has, in spite of some fluctuations and temporary difficulties eventually attained.

In 1832, under the government of Sir Wilmot Horton,
raja-karia,—or the power of employing the unpaid labor
of the peasantry of Ceylon, on public works, was formally renounced by the crown.

In 1833, the monopoly of the cinnamon trade was also
relinquished by the government, and every one who saw
fit to do so, was henceforth at liberty to cultivate, buy,
or sell that article.

What is commonly known by the name of " the charter of '33," was granted to the island by the king of
England, whereby the judicial establishments were placed on a more equitable and satisfactory footing than
before.   Trial by jury had already been introduced so
early as 1811, mainly by the instrumentality of the
Chief Justice, Sir Alexander Johnstone.

The legislative council was also inaugurated in the
same year as the charter.   In 1834, the school commission was established, with a view of promoting and
extending education in the island ; and in 1836 the
Colombo academy was first opened.   In 1837, during
the able administration of the Right Honorable Stewart

Mackenzie, the fish tax was abolished. Mr. Mackenzie was succeeded in 1841, by Sir Colin Campbell, and it was during his period of government that coffee planting received its greatest impetus : police courts and courts of requests were established, slavery entirely abol. ished, and a bishop appointed for the island, which had previously been included within the diocese of Madras. In 1847, Viscount Torrington succeeded Sir Colin Campbell. The financial embarrassments consequent upon over speculation, and the great failures of Europe in 1848, brought on a monetary crisis in Ceylon, and reduced it to the verge of bankruptcy. It was accord. ingly resolved, to impose additional taxes upon the people ; but these measures caused considerable dissatisfaction, and a rebellion broke out in the Kandian provinces, to which allusion was briefly made before : the town of Matele was plundered by the insurgents, July 28th 1848, and two days later, the town of Kurnegalle was also attacked ; but a party of the Ceylon rifles arrived just in time to save it from pillage ; the rebels were in a very short time defeated wherever they ventured to show themselves, and martial law having been declared throughout the disaffected districts, numerous military executions took place, and the rebellion was completely put down : an obscure individual had been brought forward as a claimant to the throne of Ceylon : he wes apprehended, tried, and sentenced to flogging, and transportation to Malacca : but died of small pox on his way to that settlement. Much difference of opinion prevailed in the island as to the expediency of the measures which preceded the rebellion, as well as to the propriety of maintaining martial law so long after

the outbreak had been suppressed. Party feeling ran
high, the whole question was brought before the house of
commons in England, and several of the public function-
aries, who were summoned to give evidence before it, were
transferred to appointments in other parts of the world.
The subject is one of too recent occurrence to admit of
being dwelt on at greater length. Let us hope that the
rebellion of 1848, may be the last Ceylon shall ever witness ; and that enjoying alike, all the rights and privileges of British subjects, the Anglo Saxon and the Ceylonese,—(we use that word in its widest and most comprehensive sense,) may go hand in hand in the endeav-
or to develop the latent resources of this lovely country,
and to raise it to that high pitch of prosperity which
it is capable of attaining.

Among the ordinances passed in 1848, that, called
the road ordinance has continued in force, and has been
one great means of contributing to the progress of the
island. It provides that every man resident in Ceylon,
between the ages of 18 and 55, with the exception of
the governor, the military, the Tamil estate coolies, and
the Budhist priests, shall be liable when called on, to
work six days in every year, on some public road within
a reasonable distance from his dwelling, or else pay an
equivalent in money for exemption from such labor.
This valuable ordinance owed its existence to Mr. P.
Wodehouse, at that time government agent of the Western Province, and recently governor of Demerara.

In 1850, Sir George Anderson succeeded Lord Torrington, and during the period of his administration all
connection between the government and the Budhist
religion was severed, and the custody of the dalada relic

transferred to a De've Nileme, in conjunction with the Budhist chief priests in Kandy. In 1855, Sir Henry Ward assumed the reins of government, and during his administration the island made rapid advances. His untiring energy led him to visit the most remote and unfrequented, as well as the most civilized parts of the country, and wherever he went his active spirit infused itself into the officers of government. Arriving also in Ceylon, at a time when a considerable amount of surplus revenue had accumulated in the public coffers, he found himself possessed of the means of carrying out those plans for internal improvement, which his judgment approved of; bridges, and public buildings sprang up on every side, roads were multiplied, some of the ancient works of irrigation were restored, and an irrigation ordinance passed. The surveyor's and civil engineer's departments were extended, the civil service placed on a more liberal footing, the pearl fishery once more yielded a return, an electric telegraph brought Ceylon into closer connection with India, a steamer was purchased to run round the island, penny postage was introduced, and a railway company inaugurated. It will be no matter of surprise, that where so much was attempted, the benefits expected to accrue, did not always follow. The railway scheme has proved a burden to the colony, hard to be borne, owing to the nature of the contract entered into with a company ; the terms of agreement were disapproved of by several members of the legislative council, and amongst others by our present governor : its nature is to some extent embarrassing; but the present government has the public confidence, and the impression seems to be that what can be done to surmount the difficulty will be done. Sir Henry Ward's administration was not faultless; but the period of his government will ever be a bright spot in the history of the island. The task of his successor will be a far more difficult one, —one, demanding peculiar qualifications; it would be unbecoming to say more than that his experience and known judgment, promise much. In the early part of 1860, Sir Henry Ward was promoted to the government of Madras, and general Lockyer, temporarily carried on the government, as commanding officer of the forces: his health failing him soon after, he left the island, and colonel C. E. Wilkinson of the royal engineers succeeded him. On the 22d October 1860, Sir Charles MacCarthy, who had previously filled the offices of auditor general, and colonial secretary, returned to the island as governor, after a visit to England.

It appears desirable, before closing this chapter, to draw a brief outline of the administrative organization of the island at the present day.

The governor of Ceylon is appointed by the queen, either from England direct, or from some other colony; the case of our present governor, who previously held office in the island, is an exceptional one. The governor is assisted by, and presides over an executive council consisting of the officer commanding the forces, the colonial secretary, the queen's advocate, the treasurer, and the auditor general. The legislative council is presided over by the governor, and is composed of the members of the executive council, the government agents for the Western and Central Provinces, the

surveyor general, the collector of sea customs, and
five unofficial gentlemen, who respectively represent the
Singhalese, Tamil, Burgher, planting, and mercantile interests. The assistant colonial secretary officiates as.
clerk to both councils.

The six provinces into which the island is divided,
are severally presided over by officers called government agents, who, with the help of younger members of
the civil service, called assistant agents, carry on the
financial administration of their provinces. | The native
headmen under their control, are their valuable and indispensable auxiliaries.

The judicial administration is entrusted to a supreme
court, composed of a chief justice and two puisne judges ;
and to district judges and magistrates, who are distributed over the island. The supreme court has original
jurisdiction over crimes of a serious nature, which are
brought before it periodically at Colombo, and on circuit,
by the queen's advocate or his deputy ; it also exercises
an appellate jurisdiction over all the minor courts. The
district courts have unlimited civil, and limited criminal
jurisdiction, subject however to appeal ; the magistrates
have civil and criminal jurisdiction in minor cases, and
as justices of the peace. take depositions in cases of a
grave nature, for the queen's advocate. The colonial
secretary, auditor general, and treasurer, have offices
in Colombo. The sea customs', civil engineer's, survey-
or's, and post master's departments, are each presided
over by one head with a staff of officers, who act
more or less under his control, at ⬛ations. The
registrar's office is an appendage of the supreme court.
The commisariat is partly a military and partly a civil

10

department.   The school commission, master atten-
dant's department, steamer agency, botanical garden,
loan office, saving's bank, medical department, and imi-
gration labor commission, make up the total of the different branches of the public service, with the exception
of the ecclesiastical, which is composed of an Anglican
bishop and clergy, besides two Scotch and two Dutch
presbyterian chaplains.

CHAPTER, V.

The Antiquities of Ceylon.

The descriptions of the public edifices and agricultural works of Ceylon in the olden times, are substantiated by the ruins that to this day remain, enveloped frequently, within the dense foliage of forests that beneath a tropic sun have sprung up around them; and after making all due allowance for oriental hyperbole, there is evidence amply sufficient to satisfy the traveller that the now solitary and unhealthy regions about Anuradhapura and Pollonnarua were once instinct with human life; that the sovereigns who successively swayed the sceptre were keenly alive to the importance of developing the resources of a grateful soil; and that the labor expended on their stupendous agricultural works brought back a return, not only sufficient to supply the wants of a teeming population, but also to enable them, while maintaining a court, the splendor of which was the theme of foreign princes, and the incentive to foreign rapacity, to spend countless sums on structures, in designing which, the idea of utility was utterly discarded, and that of grandeur alone entertained.

RUINS OF EDIFICES.

We begin with those of the more ancient capital. Every where about Anuradhapura, the sculptured records of its former splendor exist. Selected by Panduwa'sa as his capital, in the sixth century before Christ, his immediate successors vied with each other in embellishing it; and according to Turnour, it was eventually enclosed by a wall, sixteen gows, or sixty four miles round, embracing an area of 244 square miles ; including doubtless, gardens as well as buildings within its compass.

The most venerable monument of antiquity is the enclosure within which stands the " Jaya Sri Maha Bodin Wahanse"—the celebrated bo tree which was brought from the kingdom of Magadha, the modern Bahar, in the third century before Christ, during the reign of the Singhalese king, Devenepiatissa, and planted where it now stands. According to the Mahawanse, Dharmasoka king of Magadha having with a vermillion pencil marked the desired place of severance on the parent tree, which was said to be that one under which Gotama attained the Budhaship, the branch spontaneously disunited itself, and was carried to Ceylon with the utmost solemnity and reverence ; numberless miracles are alleged to have been performed during its transit and subsequent planting where it now stands.

Rejecting the supernatural parts of the narrative, there is every reason for believing that the antiquity of the tree has been correctly stated : though now upwards of two thousand years old, it is still fresh and healthy. Succeeding sovereigns adorned the spot where it was planted, and it stands at the present day, a silent but most interesting witness of ages gone by.

Among the dagobas about Anuradhapura, deserving of special notice, the first in point of antiquity is the Thuparamaya, a monument enclosing as it is said, the right jaw bone of Gotama. It was built by Devenepiatissa in the third century before Christ, and is 70 feet in height. Some of the classic stone pillars, with elegantly chiselled capitals, which surrounded it, are still in existence.

Next in antiquity, and far superior in size and magnificence, was the Ruanwelli dagoba, commenced by Dutugaimunu, B. C. 160, and completed by his successor. It sustained much injury during a Tamil inroad, A. D. 1214. It is now 150 feet high, and is built of brick : a subterranean passage formerly led to the interior.

Not far from the sacred bo tree, the eye is arrested by a number of stone pillars, some standing, others fallen, or as if about to fall. These are the pillars of the famous Lowa Maha Paya, or brazen palace of Dutugaimunu, so called, because the roof was covered with that metal. It was built in the second century before Christ, as a residence for the priests, and was supported by sixteen hundred pillars. In their present rough condition, these pillars fail to suggest any idea of beauty : particularly when compared with the graceful columns of Mehintalai or the Thuparamaya. It is however more than probable that they were in former times covered with cement, and adorned with precious substances. It is related in the Mahawanse, page 163, that the king "caused a gilt hall to be constructed in the middle of the palace." "The hall was supported on golden pillars representing lions and other animals, as well as the de'wata's. At the extremity of the hall it was ornamented with festoons of pearls, and all around with beads."

"In this supreme palace there were nine stories, and in each of them one hundred apartments. All these apartments were highly embellished ; they had festoons of beads resplendant like gems. The flower ornaments appertaining thereto were also set with gems, and the tinkling festoons were of gold. In that palace there were a thousand dormitories having windows with ornaments (like unto) jewels, which were bright as eyes."

Such is part of the description of the famous brazen palace, a testimony both of the munificence of its erecter and his reverence for the priesthood. It is specially recorded that the laborers employed in its construction were remunerated; the king being of opinion that " on this occasion it was not fitting to exact unpaid labor ;" from which it may fairly be inferred that it was generally the practice to employ compulsory labor, probably that of the aborigines ; and this may account for the satisfaction with which the Gangetic race regarded the construction of public edifices—a feeling that would probably not have existed had their own efforts been taxed.

The Abha'yagiri dagoba was erected by Walagam Bahu 1st, B. C. 87, on his rescuing the throne from the usurpation of the Tamils. It was originally no less than 180 cubits in height, but is now reduced to 240 feet. The Suwana ra'maya dagoba was erected by the same king. The Jaytawana'ra'ma dagoba was built by Mahasen in the third century after Christ. It was 210 feet in height, and its circumference is still 1080 feet. It is surrounded by a spacious court paved with stone, and it has been estimated, (according to Sir E. Tennent,) that the whole mass contains twenty millions of cubic feet.

About eight miles from Anuradhapura, in an easterly direction, a hill suddenly rises above the plain. A flight of a thousand steps, partly built, partly cut out of the solid rock, leads to a stone dagoba ; and ascending still farther, the traveller finds himself at the base of a second dagoba of brick. This remarkable hill is called

Mahintalai, in honor of Mahindo, the founder of Budhism in Ceylon. The lower, or Ambustulla dagoba is supposed to mark the exact spot where the meeting took place between Mahindo, and king Devenepiatissa. The upper dagoba, called the Ambhalato, is said to enshrine a single hair from the forehead of Budha.

Between Mahintalai and Kandy, at a distance of fortyfive miles from the latter place, is a huge mass of gneiss which towers above the level country to the height of 350 feet. The name of the place is Dambool, and the caves in the side of the rock have been converted into Budhist temples, and at the present day glow with all the brightness of coloring the painter's art can bestow. On entering a richly carved gateway, an image of Budha is discovered in a sitting position, and within, is a figure " in a reclining posture 40 feet in length." (Sir E. Tennent.) This temple was first endowed by Walagam Bahu, B. C. 86. It is still a place of much resort, and when in 1855, the writer inspected it on his way from Anuradhapura, in company with one of the few European ladies who have ever visited these spots, crowds of pilgrims of both sexes, dressed in their gayest attire, were swarming up and down the sides of the well worn rock.

We next proceed to Pollonnarua, the more recent capital of the island, situated on the banks of an extensive tank. No scene " (says Sir Emerson Tennent)" can be conceived more impressive than this beautiful city must have been in its pristine splendor ; the stately buildings stretching along the shore of the lake, their gilded cupolas reflected on its still expanse, and embowered in the dense foliage of the surrounding forests. At

the present day it is by far the most remarkable asse a
blage of ruins in Ceylon, not alone from the number
and dimensions, but from the architectural superiority of its buildings."

Pollonnarua had been a favorite residence of royalty
so early as A. D. 718. It was however Mahindo 1st who
about the year 775 abandoned the ancient capital and
adopted it as the seat of government.   It was here that
Prakrama Bahu the magnificent was crowned A. D. 1153,
and he it was that raised it to the height of its splendor.
According to the Mahawanse it was seven gows or 28 miles
long, and 4 gows broad, the whole surrounded by a wall.
Prakrama enlarged the lake, erected numerous edifices,
and planted gardens.   The Rankot dagoba was built by
his queen.   It is 558 feet in circumference and 186 in
height.   The main street of the city, which formed the
approach to this monument, may (according to Sir E.
Tennent,) be still traced by the foundations of the houses
that lined it on either side.

Farther up the street is the Jaytu Wana Rama temple, built by the king, on a model it is said, of one erected at Kapilewasta by Gotama himself.   It differs in
character from Singhalese structures generally, and the
workmen employed on it were brought over from India.
It contains a gigantic image of Budha.   Not far from
it is the King dagoba, so called from its milklike white-
ness.   It was surmounted by a golden spire, and was
built A. D. 1187.   Near it are some stone pillars which
mark the site where the gam sabawe or town council
was wont to assemble.

The Galwihara is said to be one of the few, if not
the only temple in the island, which is sculptured out of
the living rock.

The remains of the royal palace testify to its having
been a splendid specimen of art. It appears to have
been built at a period later than that of Prakrama Bahu,
and is supposed to owe its existence to Wijayo Bahu 3d,
on the restoration of Pollonnarua after a Malabar invasion, in the 13th century.

The Sat Mahal Pasada, or seven storied house, still
exists ; and in front of it is the Galpota, or stone book,
shaped to resemble an ola book. It is 26 feet long, 44
broad, and 2 thick ; and it bears an inscription to the
effect that king Nissanga's strong men brought it from
Mahintelai, a distance of 80 miles. Near it is the Delada
Maligawa, which held the sacred tooth.

In a former part of this work, allusion was made to
king Kasyappa, who after the murder of his father, fortified himself within the rock Sigiri, a contraction of Si-
ha-giri, or the lion rock. This remarkable hill shoots up
perpendicularly 400 feet from the plain ; it was surrounded with a rampart by the parricide, and a flight of
stone steps led to his place of retreat. Tradition says
that on the summit a tank existed ; but no one has in
later times ventured to test the truth of the story.

The last, though by no means the least ancient or interesting dagoba we shall speak of, is the one at Bintenne, in the Badulla district. The city itself was of extreme
antiquity ; according to Sir E. Tennent, it was the Maa-
grammum of Ptolemy, and a city of the Yakkos ;
and it was here that Gotama to have first set foot
in Ceylon. Its ancient name was Maharangana, and it
was built on the banks of the Mahavilleganga. So late
as 1602 the city was still in a flourishing condition ; and
the Dutch Admiral Spelbergen passed through it on his

way to Kandy. The dagoba was built three hundred years before Christ, by the brother of king Devene-piatissa. " It is a huge semi-circular mound of brick work, three hundred and sixty feet in circumference, and still one hundred feet high, but so much decayed at the top that its original outline is no longer ascertainable." Sir E. Tennent.

Such are the principal edifices to be met with among the ruined cities of Ceylon. Space will not permit us to dwell at greater length on the elaborate carvings and sculpturings still in existence, though manifesting as they do, considerable acquaintance with the fine arts. The feelings of the spectator in contemplating these relics of a by-gone age, are of a mingled character. Calculated apparently to resist for ever the ravages of decay, they have crumbled away beneath the insidious influences of a foe, from which danger would scarcely have been expected. The tiny seed dropped between the crevices of the masonry by some bird, as it rested for a while in its course, has germinated—it has insinuated its roots within the structure—increasing in size it has rent the mass asunder, and the work of destruction once begun, has advanced more and more rapidly with each succeeding year. As vegetation has encroached on the once thickly peopled city, sickness has followed in its train: a heavy oppressive air broods over all—a rank undergrowth springs around. The already scanty population becomes less—the feeble succumb, the survivers flee—the wild beasts roam amidst the deserted halls of princes—the elephant browses at will beside the giant statue of Budha. Silence and desolation reign supreme; and a few sickly, fever stricken inhabitants scattered here and there in hamlets, and an ignorant priest or two, gliding, in yellow robes amidst the colossal monuments of the past, are all that remain to represent the ancient grandeur of the spot.

WORKS OF IRRIGATION.

In one of the earliest of his minutes, Sir Henry Ward says, that branching off from the main road to Trincoma-lie, about six miles from Dambool, he met with no less than nine tanks within a distance of sixty miles. In the course of his investigation he found that they were con-structed "with great labor, considerable engineering skill, and of such solidity, that their embankments seemed to defy the hand of time. North of these again, about forty miles, is Paduvil colum, the most gigantic work of all, for the bund, which is in perfect repair except at the one spot where in the course of ages the waters have forced a passage between it and the natural hills which it united, is eleven miles long, thirty feet broad at the summit, one hundred and sixty feet at the base, and seventy feet high : and that to the westward of Pa-duvil colum again, lie the tank of Anuradhapura and the giant's tank, the dimensions of which I cannot give, as the work was never completed according to the original design."

" Paduvil colum great part of which I walked or rode over, was formed by the water of the rivers Morra oya and Moongamo oya, confined plain by the enor-mous bund which I have just described. Its construc-tion must have occupied a million of people for 10 or 15 years."

" The tank when full is said to have irrigated the whole

space between the bund and the sea, in the direction of
Kokelai. A vast breach is now open, the depth of which
is said to be unfathomable; and what was once the basin
of the tank is covered with magnificent timber, except in
those parts which are still under water during the rainy
season. These are overgrown with a coarse rank grass;
for miles around, there is not a vestige of man, and the
temporary building erected for our reception had the effect of frightening away all the game in the country, so
unaccustomed were the deer and buffaloes which frequent
the tank to any intrusion upon their solitudes." (Sir
Henry Ward.)

The nine tanks between Dambool and Trincomalie,
alluded to above, are those of Sigiri, Kondruwewe, An-
goulassa, Dimitelle, Pollonnarua or Topari, Giritelle,
Minere, Kowdelle, and Kandelle or Gantalawe.

There can be no doubt that a perfect net work of canals connected the different tanks; that every river or
stream that could be turned to account was intercepted,
its waters diverted into these huge reservoirs, and there
husbanded, by the aid of artificial embankments, generally stretched between two hills, and constructed,—
where such a measure appeared necessary, of massive
blocks of stone, artistically bevilled in such a manner
that pressure only consolidated them the more firmly;
furnished with sluices and spill waters for the irrigation
of the surrounding f   and the escape of the surplus
water. At the time   these works were common
throughout the island, the art of irrigation was in Europe in its rudest state; and no oriental Cotton had yet
spanned the Kavery and Colleroon by anicuts, and converted Tanjore into a garden of unceasing fertility.

The work to which we first propose directing our atten-
tion, is the Ellahara canal, which Messrs Bailey,
Churchill, and Adams, succeeded in tracing from the
Matelo district to the neighborhood of Trincomalie.

The Ellahara canal was commenced by king Mahasen
A. D. 275. It was fed by the waters of the Karaganga,
a river which the gentlemen before named have identified with the Ambanganga of Matele. This river fed
the various tanks in its course, including those of Minery
and Kowdelle, the first of which is 21 miles in circumference · the second, though now in ruins, its bed being
covered by forest trees, is said to have been 37 miles
round. Although the canal · was commenced by
Mahasen, the original design was extended and considerably improved by king Prakrama Bahu 2nd, A.
D. 1153. By constructing a bund at Ellahara, he diverted the waters of the Karaganga into what is called
the " sea of Prakrama," an expanse of water formed
by a series of extensive tanks connected with each other
by canals, It would be difficult to say what extent of
country was thus converted into an inland "sea ;" but
some idea may be formed of the magnitude of the under-
taking when it is stated that one of the embankments
alone, stretches along a distance of 24 miles, and varies
in height from 40, to 90 feet. To follow more at length
the interesting report of the explorers, and to repeat
their description of the hewn stor 'ocks, masonry work,
spill waters, sluices, &c. wor   'beyond our limits :
suffice it to say that they succeeded in tracing the Ellahara canal to Kandelle near Trincomalie, where that
lake pours its surplus waters into the sea at Tamblegam
bay, which is itself believed to have at one time been

11

an extensive tank, into which the sea forced its way. The locality of the famed "sea of Prakrama," which had previously been a matter of uncertainty, has now been determined; it has also been satisfactorily ascertained that in ancient times boats from the vicinity of Trincomalie navigated the Ellahara canal; and a tree was pointed out by the natives as the "tamarind tree to which the boats used to be tied."

The Anuradhapura tank, though not the most important, is the oldest work of its kind. It was constructed by Panduwa'sa, in the fifth century before Christ.

The giant's tank, in the Manaar district, is so called because the huge masses of rock forming the lower part of its dam, which are said to have sustained no injury by time, were supposed to have been hewn and carried to their places by giants. To whom the design is due, of attempting to collect and confine a mass of water as extensive as the lake of Geneva, is unknown. In order to feed this tank, it was intended to divert from its course the Aripo river, the tributaries of which alone are often formidable streams. The attempt proved abortive, for, after all the vast expenditure of labor, the evidences of which continue to this day, it was found that the levels had been wrongly taken; and the courtly chroniclers, unwilling to record royal failures have refrained from naming the sovereign in whose reign this work was under   n. The giant's tank now contains within its basin   villages which have sprung up since its formation.

A companion piece to the giant's tank, is that of Kaleweva, between Anuradhapura and Dambool, which Turnour calls "one of the most stupendous monuments

of misapplied human labor existing." It was improved
if not constructed by king Dhatu Sena, by drawing an
embankment across the Kalu Oya, A. D. 460. The bund
is twelve miles long, and the spill water is of hewn
granite. The waters thus confined were thrown back
for twenty miles to the foot of the Dambool rock, where
a canal sixty miles long connected the lake with the
city of Anuradhapura : but the waters burst the embankments, and rendered the work useless.

The Horra-borra tank in Bintenne, is the last work
of the kind, which we shall notice, on which no modern
effort has been expended. An artificial embankment
200 feet broad, has here been drawn across a river, at
a spot where two masses of rock rising from the bed of
the stream add solidity to the work. These rocks, though
sixty feet in thickness, have been tunnelled so as to al-
low the surplus water to escape through them ; they
were formerly fitted with sluice gates, and the waters
arrested by the embankment were thrown back a distance
of eight or ten miles.

The restoration of these ancient sources of wealth has
frequently been the subject of speculation : we venture to
state as our opinion that not only do the conditions under
which they were originally constructed, no longer exist,
but also that any attempts to renew them, except under
peculiarly favorable circumstances and in particular lo-
calities would be impracticable ; and that even under the
most favorable circumstances the success of the experi-
ment would be dubious. Although the Mahawanse is to a
great degree silent on the subject, passages occur here
and there to further the belief that however mild and be-
nignant were the laws for the government of the domi-

nant race, the aborigines held a subordinate, if not a servile position. It would appear that they were the forced labor- ers by whose toil the public works were principally con- structed. Experience has in modern times amply shewn that not even the prospect of certain and immediate ad. vantage to their property, has been sufficient to overcome the reluctance of the Singhalese to repair or improve the channels which irrigate their lands; and even under the pressure of the irrigation ordinance, passed to en- force their doing that, which self interest should have prompted them to do spontaneously, it has been found dif- ficult to rouse them to exertion. When in view of this, we consider the plaudits bestowed by the people in former times, on those kings who extended works of irrigation requiring a vast amount of time and labor, and when we remember how it is especially recorded that a king on *one* occasion paid for the labor of the Yakkos, and further when we bear in mind how it was always the practice in olden times for the conquerors to make their conquer- ed subjects hewers of wood and drawers of water, the supposition we have hazarded is materially strengthen- ed. Such a condition of things we can never wish or expect again to see : and without free labor, no govern. ment could undertake such works as the ancient tanks, at any time, still less in the present day, when the cul- tivation of rice, under the most favorable circumstances is the least remuner（ ̣ of any cultivation in the island. To all appearance, th ̣ lories of Anuradhapura and Pol- lonnarua, of Paduvil culum, the sea of Prakrama, and Mineri, are for ever departed ; or, if the forests that en- velop them shall again echo with the sound of the axe or the crash of falling timber, the Anglo Saxon must lead

the van, and his object must be other than the growth
of grain. There are resources lying hidden in those
leafy depths, worth more than paddy : there are productions better able to bear taxation, which have already
engaged the attention of the people ; and he who shakes
the traditional belief in the advantages of sinking money
in jewels, stone houses, and paddy fields, and directs
the energies of the native in the remoter parts of the island
towards coffee, tobacco, cotton, cocoanuts, &c. will do a
good work, and one that will bring its own reward.
Where men already hold ancestral fields, and where they
can find no other outlet for their labor, there, it is desirable to encourage the growth of rice, and even to aid and
direct them in husbanding the water on which they must
rely for a return. But it is folly for people to pay forty and
fifty pounds per acre for paddy fields, which under the
most favorable circumstances, cannot yield any thing like
the percentage that might have been derived by simply
laying out the money on interest.

During the administration of Sir Henry Ward, the
tanks of Errecamum and Ambare, in the Eastern Province, and that of Oroobokka, in the Southern have
been restored.

CHAPTER, VI.

Religion, Literature, Education.

RELIGION.

Concerning the religion of the ancient inhabitants of Ceylon little is known. They are supposed to have worshipped snakes and demons; and it is probable that the devil dances, which, though not in accordance with Budhism, are prevalent amongst the Singhalese, and which at present are the only approach to religious worship amongst the Veddahs, have been perpetuated since their time.

The religion of the mass of Singhalese is Budhism : of the Tamils, " Hinduism," a word which we are compelled to force into our service, for want of a better. With both, Christianity has made more or less progress. The Moormen are almost without exception Mohamedans.

Gotama Budha, who revived, if he did not found Budhism, was born of royal parents at Patna in the kingdom of Magadha, or as it is now called, Bahar, B. C. 624. Wonderful instances of precocity are related of him. When only 5 months old, he is said to have sat in the air without support, and the soothsayers predicted his future eminence. At sixteen he married, and in time became the father of a son. It had been foretold that the sight of four things would in **·e** the coming Budha to renounce the world. They we**··** decrepitude, sickness, death, and a recluse. His father in vain sought to guard Gotama from coming into proximity with these : and the sight of the last having inspired him with an unconquerable desire to adopt a similar mode of existence, he bade adieu to the charms of wedded life, and after one glance at his infant while sleeping in the arms of its mother, quitted his regal home and retired into solitude. Practicing the most austere asceticism, after having reduced his daily allowance of food to the quantity containable in a pepper pod, he sank exhausted at the foot of a spreading bo tree, and there attained the supreme Budhaship. All the efforts of malignant demons to disturb his serenity proved abortive, and before his reproving look they vanished as the clouds from before the moon : henceforth he possessed a power that could accomplish, and a wisdom that could understand all things. He now commenced his ministrations, visiting various parts of India as well as Ceylon ; he also occasionally betook himself to other worlds. After many proofs of his greatness he died at the age of eighty. The place of his death is uncertain, some alleging it was Delhi and others Assam : his remains were burnt and such relics as were preserved, or supposed to have been preserved, are adored by his followers.

According to the tenets of Budha, wisdom and virtue are the two objects to be sought after. Supreme excellence consists in the extinction of all desire. Those who fail to attain this, continue to pass from one state of existence to another. As one lamp is kindled from another, so is it with the successive conditions of the individual. If so fortunate as eventually to overcome all desire, the lamp burns out and existence ceases. This condition is called *Nirwana*, or the absence of desire ; and this is all that Budhism can offer its followers as the reward of the most rigid asceticism. To *be*, is to *suffer*, to cease to *be*, is to cease to *suffer*. According to this doctrine, Gotama Budha, is *not*. He has ceased to exist. His doctrines remain, his memory is revered, his example followed, his image adored. But he is not worshipped as a Divine Being, controlling the affairs of the world, and capable of rewarding and punishing. The Budhist has literally no God. Merit and demerit, according to his philosophy, necessarily produce fruit after their kind. There is no recognition of propitiation, pardon, or atonement. Cause and effect are absolute, but the effect may follow after the individual has passed through several ages of being, and he may be perfectly ignorant of the cause. It is by no means uncommon for a Budhist on being plunged into misfortune, to say " this must be on account of some sin committed by me in a former birth." As a natural consequence of the belief, —not of transmigration exactly, but rather of the renewal of existence under various forms, the destruction of animal life is forbidden. Even the priests however will partake of meat if the animal was not killed by themselves or at their instigation.*

Gotama was not the only Budha; many existed before him, and he specially alludes to six. Budhas are persons who in each successive stage of existence have gone on acquiring more and more merit, and more and more lost desire of every kind. Pleasure

---

*An amusing tale is related illustrative of this. Curried wild pig was a favorite dish of one of the Kandian kings. Whenever it appeared on the board however, his majesty professed great indignation at this violation of Budhistical tenets, until assured that it had been recovered from the claws of a cheeta, which had seized and killed it. The royal scruples having been thus satisfied, the king was accustomed to fall to, with the gusto of an ordinary individual.

and pain, the social relations, the appetites, the emotions of the mind have lost all influence over them ; they become indifferent to all things sublunary, and are wrapped in meditation. Their last condition is always that of man ; on attaining the Budhaship they manifest its acquisition by miracles, until existence ceases. Those persons who do not become Budhas, but subdue their passions and extinguish their desires, are called Rahats. Budhism has been embraced by no less than one-third of the human race. It extends over Thibet, Nepal, China, Burma, Siam, and Japan. It was introduced into Ceylon in the fourth century before Christ.

Although Budhism, according to the teaching of its founder, is what has been described above, many innovations have crept in. There is in the heart of man, a disposition to worship some Being; and this disposition is apt to degenerate into the worship of more than one. The abstract refinements of Budhism are not understood by the vulgar ; and the learned find it useless to endeavor to enlighten them. Having no god of their own, they adopt those of others ; and the Hindu deities, Vishnu and Shiva, are generally to be found side by side with the placid image of Budha.

As virtue and wisdom are the objects of their reverence, they even give Christianity, whose founder they admit to have possessed these qualities in a preeminent degree, a place in their system.

The Budhist priests professedly devote themselves to a life of abstinence. If married, the neophyte quits his family, assumes the yellow robe, causes his head, beard, and eye-brows to be shorn, and directs his attention to the subjugation of self, and the study of the sacred books.

If he find this self imposed task too difficult, he is at liberty to renounce the robes and return to society.

The priests generally reside in buildings in the vicinity of the temple, or *Wihari*, in which the images of Budha are erected. The character of these residences which are called *Pansalas*, corresponds in many respects with the monasteries of Europe. A writer in a late number of the quarterly review, who endeavors to trace the ruins of Stonehenge to a Budhist origin, and to identify the god Woden or Wod with Bodh or Budh, draws attention to several striking points of resemblance between the monastic institutions of Europe and those of Asia, and suggests that the latter were the models of the first.

Mendicancy, as well as celibacy, is one of the requirements of a priest. There were in former times convents for priestesses or female devotees, but these no longer exist.

HINDUISM.

If Budhism denies the existence of a God, Hinduism counts its deities by hundreds of millions. The contrast between the two systems is as great in other respects.

Budhism throws open the treasures of its sacred lore to all. Hinduism most jealously guards them from the masses.

Budhism admits all classes to the priesthood. Hinduism recognises but one divinely born order.

Budhism ignores caste. Hinduism regards it as its life blood.

Budhism demands celibacy of its priests. Hinduism does not.

Budhism is latitudinarian and affiliative. Hinduism is conservative and exclusive.

The doctrines of Hinduism are contained in the Veds and Puranas. The first lay claim to an antiquity coeval with the birth of the favored caste of Brahmins who are their depositaries. Written in the Sanskrit, a language unknown to the vulgar, they are still further guarded from profane scrutiny by the most terrible denunciations,—the Brahmins, the royal race, and the Chetties being alone allowed to peruse them. These books profess to inculcate not only the most sublime truths that language can express, but to regulate and control the most minute actions of man's daily life ; his uprising and his down sitting, his eating and his drinking, his washing and his clothing, the observances at his birth, his marriage, his death and his funeral; and so minute and multifarious are the rules prescribed, that it has been calculated no single lifetime is long enough to master them all.

The mystery in which these highly lauded works was so long enveloped has however to some extent been cleared away. The researches of students have shewn that their professed antiquity has been over-rated, and parts of the *rigvetham* have moreover been translated into the vernacular by professor Wilson, and published in the English language.

According to the *vetham* there is one supreme, universal, and self-existent intelligence called Brahm, by whom the universe was brought into existence. His transcendental character raises him above the comprehension of mortals, and he is exalted infinitely too high to occupy himself in any degree with the work of his creation. Hence no temples are erected in honor of him, and no worship of any kind is offered to him. From Brahm, proceeded the Hindu Triad,—Brahma the Creator—Vishnu the preserver—and Sivun the destroyer. Each of the two latter has his own temples and devotees who claim the supremacy for the deity who is the peculiar object of their adoration, and who in point of fact form separate sects, agreeing on some general subjects, such as caste, and the superiority of the Brahmins, but differing very widely on many other points. To Brahma it is said that there is only one temple in all India, and even this statement is doubtful. May not the reason of this be, that with the Hindu, fear, not love, is the actuating principle. Hence the Sivite invokes Sivan because he can destroy, and the Vishnuite Vishnu, because he can preserve. But Brahma in creating, completed his task; an offering to him can neither secure favor nor avert evil—and therefore to make one, would be a useless expenditure.

It is from Brahma that all sentient being proceeds. From his head emanated the Brahmins, while simultaneously his lips gave utterance to those oracles of which they are the custodians. From his arm and breast sprang the military, from his thighs the mercantile and agricultural orders; and from his feet, the humble Shudras. The idea of all men being of one blood, in our acceptation of the term, is indignantly scouted by the Hindu: and whatever may have been the idea of caste entertained by the early founders of the Brahminical system, it is at the present day one of the most prominent features of Hinduism. The individual who by accident or design forfeits his caste, is looked upon with loathing and abhorrence by his nearest relatives. His mother, his children, and his wife, shrink from contact with him, and he stands alone, without friend or associate. To a Hindu, such a condition is worse than death. In some cases however, under peculiar circumstances, he is allowed to undergo a purification that restores him to the once lost position.

It is incorrect to say, as some do, in extenuation of caste, that its principle prevails amongst Europeans. We have it is true, lines of social demarcation, but no religious feeling regulates their bounds. The instances are numerous in which men of humble birth have raised themselves to positions of eminence, and secured an honored place at the table and council board of royalty. The celebrated Wolsey for instance, was the son of a butcher. Noblemen too of the highest rank, and even members of the royal family are not unfrequently entertained at public banquets by persons far below them in the social scale; such as the fish mongers' company, the goldsmiths' company, the cloth merchants' company, &c. But the poorest Brahmin, if orthodox, would consider himself, and be considered by others for ever degraded, and lose his caste, were he to partake of one morsel of food at the table of Queen Victoria. In Jaffna however, and other parts of the island where religious education has made progress, there is reason to believe that the influence of the Brahmins has been much weakened. Caste too, though still rigid on some points, has been found capable of being made to stretch, and experience justifies the assertion that where the sacrifice of any custom is firmly demanded, and it is the interest of the individual to yield, he will in nine cases out of ten do so; we may foster caste by tenderness or strangle it by resolution. It is however Protean in its forms, and will long continue to lift up its head when we think it dead. The only way is to hit it whenever it shews itself.

As to the influence of the Brahminical priesthood, the insinuation of its office into every transaction of life, and its demands on the offerings of the people, it may be said that it is generally felt to be a burden they would willingly shake off if they knew how : but no body likes to begin. Like Sindbad the sailor, and the old man, who, having once succeeded in inducing Sindbad to take him on his back, refused to get down again, so is it with the Brahmin and the people. But Sindbad eventually contrived to shake off the encumbrance, and then walked free and erect; when will the analogy be complete ?

Though there is much about its pageants and its voluptuous dances, to captivate the mind and enslave the passions, the *educated* as a body are indifferent to Hinduism. With some who have not made an open profession of religion, there is reason to believe that the doctrines of Christianity are recognized by the understanding ; but the solicitations of friends and the love of gain prove too powerful, and they hold back. Others have nominally adopted Christianity, because their hope of profit lies in that direction, and are despised by both parties. Some there are again, who have taken hold of it from real conviction; who have withstood the endeavors of relatives to draw them back, and lead consistent lives.

Although we have briefly described Hinduism in its popular form, we must remember that there is beneath its surface, a philosophy of a very much more profound character. The writings of their ancient sages, though the productions of men groping in the dark, manifest deep thought, and are in a great degree free from the idolatry of the present day.

Hindu Philosophy has three systems, the Nya'ya, the Sa'nkhya, and the Veda'nta. The Nya'ya recognises five elements, earth, water, fire, air, and ether, which are supposed to bear an analogy to the five senses of man. All action necessarily causes suffering ; and the great aim of man should therefore be, to cease to act. This can only be effected by the contemplation and pursuit of wisdom ; and when the mind has abstracted itself from every thing material, and the body has ceased to exercise any sway, then suffering ends and transmigration no longer occurs.

The Sa'nkhya system rejects all dogmas, and even refuses to accept the *vethams* themselves, unless reason acquiesces. The great object of attainment is the power of discriminating between that which is material and that which is spiritual. For the soul to cease to have any connection with what is material, and consequently to cease to transmigrate, is the great good to be sought.

The Veda nta system holds that all around us is an illusion ;—that " we are such stuff as dreams are made of"—that what *seems* to be, is *not ;* that there is no world, no matter : all is God. The philosopher first brings his mind to believe that all he sees is the one great Being ; he next proceeds to identify himself with that Being : as the next step, he ceases to consider even himself; and all that remains is a *consciousness* Such, in a few words, are the systems prevalent in India. In Ceylon however, the Veda'ntic is the only one of the three, recognized ; and a fourth system called Siva Sittantism prevails there. Its followers acknowledge the existence of three eternal entities ; deity,—soul,—and matter.

Whatever differences there may be between these systems of philosophy, they all agree in regarding what-ever is practical, as unworthy the attention of the philo-sopher, nay even opposed to the attainment of future happiness ; if mere freedom from suffering can be so call-ed. A philosophy of such a character is fatal to progress. The nation that possesses a Baconian, must ever be ahead of one that possesses a purely speculative philosophy. Bacon died of a cold taken while experimenting on a dead fowl he was stuffing with ice. Franklin flew a kite into the clouds. Sir Humphrey Davy occupied himself with the construction of a lamp. The Hindu sage, with emaciated body, folded hands, and legs crossed, turns his eyes from such sublunary vanities ; tries to forget he be-longs to earth ; and despises the man that can des-cend to such trifles. But Bacon's system of induction once recognized and adopted, has given the world an impetus that carries the Hindu along with it in spite of himself ;—Franklin's kite brought the lightning from the skies, which now puts " a girdle round the earth in forty minutes," and connects the remotest coun-tries ; and Davy's safety lamp has saved the lives of thousands. The man who diverts the Oriental mind from what is speculative and directs it to what is practical, will confer an inestimable boon on society : and as " many an error would never have thriven but for learn-ed refutation," our answer to those who ask " how shall we meet the Nya'ya the Sa'nkaya and the Veda'ntic sys-tems," is, " do not uttempt to do so"—acquaint yourselves with them if you like ; but do not trouble yourselves to refute them. They may be very transcendental, and seem very learned, but they are worthless: for all they can do, is to unfit a man to be a man. A doctor may spend hours in trying to prove that the best thing for fever is something else than the preparations used by native practitioners : but a dose or two of quinine will speak more to the purpose than all he can say : and though a Hindu does not know of induction as a system, still, (as Macaulay has so admirably shewn,) the process of mental induction is intuitive and as old as the human race. That the Singhalese and the Tamils can be led to the practical, and become proficient in what is of real benefit to man, we have ample proofs ; but they become so, in spite of their philosophy, and by the force of Anglo Saxon influence.

CHRISTIANITY.

The first mention made of Christianity in Ceylon, is by Cosmos Indopleustes, a Nestorian who lived in the 6th century, during the reign of the emperor Justinian. He alludes to a colony of Christians, who were probably Nestorians, sojourning in the island for purposes of trade, and not natives. There is a legend that the apostle Thomas visited Ceylon, and that the Ethiopean Eunuch, minister of queen Candace, preached there. But these statements are unsubstantiated.

Soon after the Portuguese had established themselves, they commenced a mission amongst the Singhalese, and found little difficulty in inducing them to graft the religion of the dominant race on their own. The first preacher amongst the Tamils of whom we have any record, was the ardent Xavier, who in 1544 preached at Manaar. The success of his ministrations has already been recorded. It was in Jaffna that the most systematic efforts at propagandism were made by the Portuguese ; the accessibility of each part of the peninsula, and the compactness of its dense population rendering it easy of subdivision into parishes. Of these, 32 were organized, and in each a substantial church and a school house were built.

On the occupation of the sea board by the Dutch, they took possession of all the Portuguese churches, prohibited their priests from preaching or teaching, made it obligatory on every candidate for public office to be baptised, and with-held certain civil privileges from all who had not undergone that rite. As a natural consequence, nominal Christians multiplied, acquainted with a few formularies, but ignorant of all besides, and secretly attached all the more, to their own religion, while abhorring the creed they were forced to profess. So deep seated was this abhorrence, that it has become hereditary, and ministers have in our day found, that heathens who would attend their services in bungalows, remained away when a church was built or restored. The attempt to crush out Roman Catholicism by punishment proved abortive, as all persecution ever will do.

On the cession of their possessions to the English, the maintenance of their religious establishments was by treaty secured to the Dutch, and their ministers continued to occupy their churches, drawing their salaries from the British government. In 1801, the number of their members was estimated by Cordiner, one of the first English chaplains who arrived in the island, at 342,000. But no sooner did the natives discover that perfect tolera-tion was the principle of the new government, than they came out in their true colors, and the Christians soon dwindled down to so small a number, that the necessity ceased for supplying the places of such of the Dutch clergy as died off; and at the same time the difficulty of finding suitable persons increased, so that eventually, many stations were abandoned or handed over to other denominations, with the consent of the Dutch consistory, who expressed themselves satisfied with the good faith that had throughout been observed towards them. At present there are but two chaplains of the Dutch Reformed church in the island, the one at Colombo, and the other at Galle. Their services are conducted in the English language. Chaplains are stationed at the principal stations in the island, whose ministrations are intended for the benefit of the public servants, civil and military, and for those who are already Christians. There is no interference with the heathen, and the work of proselytism is entirely left to private effort. At the same time all proper encouragement is given to the voluntary efforts of missionaries.

As the Roman Catholics were first in the field, we speak of them first as regards missionary labor. They have established themselves in each of the six provinces into which the island is divided, and have built churches in many hamlets, as well as in the principal towns. There was a section, which, refusing to acknowledge the authority of the "Vicars Apostolic" appointed by the Pope, recognized the Portuguese arch-bishop of Goa, as their spiritual head ; and were consequently designated "the schismatics." A *concordat* has however been recently concluded between the Pope, and the sovereign of Portugal, with the view of putting an end to these divisions. There are two Bishops in the island, appointed from Rome, the one at Colombo, the other at Jaffna. The Roman Catholics have been very successful amongst the fishing classes. On the renunciation of the fish tax, the Roman Catholic converts made over the whole of what they would have had to pay to government, to their church, and have continued to do so, ever since.

Of the Protestant missions now in the island, the first in point of time were the Baptists. In 1804, three Germans were sent out by the London Missionary Society, but they did not continue long, and that body has no footing here. In 1812 a deputation from the Baptist mission at Serampore near Calcutta commenced a mission in Colombo.

In 1814, Dr. Coke of the Wesleyan body was impelled by a desire to found a mission in Ceylon, so powerful as to induce him to offer £6000 out of his private fortune to carry out the purpose. He embarked with a few others, but he was not permitted to see the dearest wish of his heart fulfilled. He died on the voyage, having attained an advanced age; his companions eventually reached Ceylon, and one of them, Harvard, has in his " narrative" gratefully acknowledged the cordiality with which they were welcomed by the members of government and all classes of the community.

In 1815, four American missionaries arrived in Colombo, and proceeded to Jaffna, where they established a mission in connection with the American Board of Foreign Missions. In 1818, the Church Mission followed In 1840, the Society for the Propagation of the Gospel entered the field, and in 1845, under the auspices of the bishop of Colombo, extended their labors in different directions.

The Baptists have adopted Colombo and Kandy as their head quarters, radiating from those two points to the surrounding districts. Amongst the names of those who have been connected with that mission, is that of the late Rev. Mr. Daniel: it is honored wherever it is mentioned. Mr. Chater, one of its earliest missionaries, published a grammar of the Singhalese language, which is still the best guide for Englishmen learning the language.

The Wesleyans, who are next in order of arrival, occupied both the Singhalese and Tamil districts. They have two chairmen, one at Colombo and one at Jaffna. They have branch stations at Negombo, Morotto, Pantura, Caltura, Galle, and Matura, in the Singhalese districts; and at Point Pedro, Trincomalie, and Batticaloa, in the Tamil districts.

The Americans have confined their operations to the north; and have taken up 17, out of the 32 parishes of Jaffna and the islands.

The Church Mission has stations at Cotta near Colombo, once the capital of the island, at Baddegame near Galle, at Kandy, and at Jaffna, where they have five parishes.

The Propagation Society has stations at Colombo, Galkisse, Morotto, Pantura, Negombo, Kandy, Puselawa, Newere Ellia, Badulla, Batticaloa, Matura, Calpentyn, Manaar, &c.

EDUCATION.

Long before Western learning had been conveyed to the East, education had been fostered and encouraged in Ceylon. King Wijayo Bahu 3rd, who lived in the 13th century after Christ, established schools in every village in the island, himself supporting the teachers. To this day, village schools are common, especially in the Tamil districts, which are wholly independent of government or mission aid.

Both the Portuguese and Dutch had schools connected with their churches, in which the formularies of their faith were taught. The English, who followed the Dutch, have placed the means of instruction within the reach of the people, without exercising any coertion, or demanding the profession of Christianity. The various missions have also employed education as an important means of effecting their end.

The government educational establishment is presided over by a board called the Central School Commission, of which the colonial secretary is the chairman. The government agent of Colombo is also an ex officio member. Clergymen of different denominations sit on it, and branch committees exist in different parts of the island.

Its principal schools, are the queen's college, formerly called the Colombo academy, which has recently been affiliated with bishop's college Calcutta; the Colombo normal institution, and the Kandy and Galle central schools.

There are four superior girls schools, of which two are in Colombo, one at Galle, and one at Kandy.

Besides these there are a number of elementary, mixed, and vernacular schools, scattered over the country. The government has recently adopted the industrial school, Colombo, heretofore connected with the Propagation Society.

Of mission schools, the first we shall mention is St.

Thomas' College, collegiate school, and orphan asylum. These three are under the immediate control of the Bishop of Colombo, and are connected with the Propagation Society, which society has moreover between 80 and 90 schools in various parts of the island.

The Church Mission has an institution of a superior character, for boys, at Cotta; a collegiate school at Kandy, a seminary for boys at Chundically; a boarding school for girls at Nellore, near Jaffna; and a vernacular institution at Copay, besides a number of village schools.

The Baptists have 27 schools in connection with their mission.

The Wesleyans have 71 schools in the Singhalese districts and 22 in the Tamil. They have a seminary for boys, and a boarding school for girls, in the town of Jaffna.

The American Mission has a female boarding school at Oodooville, about five miles from Jaffna, and 45 vernacular schools. The Batticotta Seminary, a boarding school for boys, once held a high position in the statistics of education. Some years since, it was considered desirable by the majority of the mission to discontinue it, and it was accordingly closed. The result was, that one of its native teachers opened a school of a similar character, the pupils paying for their education. It has maintained a very fair position up to this day, and the example has been followed in other places. A vernacular training and theological institution, has within the last two years been opened at Batticotta, by the American Mission.

The Roman Catholics have amongst other schools, a male and female boarding institution in Jaffna.

It would be a pleasing task to the writer, and it re-
quires some self restraint, to refrain from enlarging on
the subject of education, and the benefits it is conferring
on the community. In qualifying the intelligent and
quick witted sons of the soil for the various walks of life
open to them; and in teaching the daughters of Ceylon
how English and American women are help mates to
their husbands and guides to their offspring, a great work
is being done. In minor matters we may desire to see
some alteration or modification:—one system may
have some advantage over another; but the disinter-
ested spectator, taking an enlarged and liberal view
of education as a whole, cannot but see with pleasure
that there is progress, social, intellectual, and religious,
and, if a true friend of the people, will wish well to those
who are bringing western science to bear on eastern
mind. He will also find that in aptitude for acquiring
knowledge, the youth of Ceylon are in no respect behind the very best of Saxon lads; while as a rule, they
are much more desirous of knowledge, and anxious to
improve. For mathematics and arithmetic they have a
wonderful aptitude. Education is generally valued, mainly as a stepping stone to promotion, but some there are
who love learning from learning's sake.

It is in Jaffna where education has most permeated
the masses; in fact there are more educated men in
need of employment than can find it. This evil will
however be greatly corrected by the system now prevalent, of demanding payment for instruction in the higher schools; by which means the social balance will be
restored. Besides supplying the government offices, as
clerks and surveyors, several of the Tamil young men

have acquired considerable proficiency in medicine and surgery, under the instructions, first, of Dr. Ward, and then of Dr. Green, both of the American Mission. Two Tamil dispensers are attached to the Jaffna hospital, an institution which is a model of its kind ; which has bestowed inestimable benefit on the community ; and which reflects the greatest credit on those entrusted with its management. Several Tamil doctors are employed in the public service, and are engaged in private practice, overcoming more and more popular prejudices against European treatment. Many young men are likewise engaged in the civil engineer's department. What formerly were the American Mission press and bookbinding establishments, have, since 1855, been entirely in the hands of natives, and this little work will testify to their skill. Many Tamils likewise fill offices in the banks, or are employed in coffee estates in the Central Province, and many have been called to the bar; shewing that however speculative may be their philosophy, they are quite capable of taking a practical turn, when properly directed and encouraged.

LITERATURE.

As each Protestant mission has either the command or the use of a press, numerous publications are from time to time issued by them, calculated both to interest and instruct. The Bible has been printed in both of the vernacular languages, and in Indo Portuguese ; tracts are freely distributed ; a monthly periodical in Singhalese, called the Lanka Nidha'na, and a Tamil newspaper called the Morning Star, have an extensive circulation, and a child's newspaper has been printed for some time past at Manepy near Jaffna, and has met with much success.

13

As to English literature, there are three newspapers published in Colombo; the Observer, the Examiner and the Times. Each appears twice a week. At Galle, a fortnightly Intelligencer is published, and a debating society in Colombo has recently issued a little magazine. Attempts have at various times been made at literary periodicals, but they have been but short lived. A detailed account of all the works published in the island since its occupation by the Portuguese, would be interesting; but our limits will not admit of giving one.

It must not however be supposed that the Singhalese of old were without a literature of their own. They possessed works on astronomy, astrology, medicine, and surgery, and had some acquaintance with botany, geometry, and electricity. The Rev. M. Hardy gives, in the Asiatic Society's journal for 1847, a list of 467 works in the Singhalese and Pali languages. Their writings were graven with a style on the leaf of the talipot or palmyra tree, a practice common at the present day. The Mahawanse, the Rajavali, and the Rajaratnacari are the most celebrated historical works of the Singhalese. Though the scene of the Ra'ma'yana, the great epic poem of the Hindus, is laid principally in Ceylon, the work itself was composed in India. There are however some writers in Ceylon who have contributed both prose and poetry, to the literature of the north.

In religion, education, and literature then, we may fairly pronounce the island to be progressive. There are natives with whom the European of cultivated taste may converse with advantage on any of these three subjects, and he will find ere he has done so long, that the advantage in point of information does not always rest with himself. Were the British to retire from Ceylon tomorrow, they might point not only to bridges, roads, and other structures, as evidences of their sojourn, but to minds built on a European foundation, and stored with European science. With such facts before us, we may cheerfully hail the future of Ceylon.

NOTE.—Under the head, " Christianity," we omitted to notice the coolie mission, Kandy, connected with the Church Mission, which, under the superintendence of the Rev. S. Hobbs, is doing much good among the coolies from India, employed on the Coffee estates.

CHAPTER, VII.

Trade and Revenue of Ceylon.

There is perhaps no British dependency where the state of the revenue is more satisfactory than in Ceylon ; nor is there, it may safely be added, any place in the east, where the condition of the people is so comfortable, —where their rights are so much regarded,—where the imposts are so light,—and where property is so equally distributed. Compared with the continent of India, how great is the contrast. If on the one hand we meet with few native *millionaries*, on the other hand we fail to encounter, to any thing like a similar extent, that abject penury,—that daily struggle for existence, so common there, where splendor and beggary jostle each other, and " pale death" need take but one short stride from the "palaces of princes to the hovels of the poor." When the lower orders in South India fail to find the means of subsistence at home, they seek them and rarely seek them in vain, in Ceylon.

We annex, below, two tables extracted from the Ceylon Almanac for this year, shewing in a compendious form, the estimated revenue and expenditure for 1861.

From the first of these tables it will be seen that the customs is the principal source of revenue. The duties on goods imported and exported are estimated at £200,000. Of the articles imported, the principal are,

From Great Britain ;—apparel, cotton goods, liquor, and metals.

From India ;—grain, curry stuffs, earthen ware, cotton goods, and brass ware.

The total amount of duty so obtained, may be estimated above, rather than below £150.000

The principal exports are,

To Great Britain;—coffee, coooanut oil; coir, and
cinnamon.*

To India ;—arrack, timber, copperah, jaggery, and
tobacco.

The total amount of duty so collected may be estimated under £50,000.

The land revenue, the sale of stamps and licences,
and of government property are the items next in importance ; the land revenue is estimated at £85,000 :
the right to retail arrack, rum, and toddy, will yield
about £77,000, and the sale of salt £66,000.

The revenue derived from the pearl fishery is fluctu.
ating and uncertain. The highest amount realized since
1826, was in the year 1859, when above £48,000 were
collected ; this year nothing is expected from this source.

The payment of the different establishments of government, and the construction of public works, are the
principal items of disbursement.

---

* Coffee is grown principally in the Central province ; the cocoanut in the maritime districts ; and cinnamon in the vicinity
of Negombo, Colombo, and Galle.

In the Peninsula of Jaffna, and in the district of Batticaloa,
Europeans have engaged in the systematic cultivation of the
coconut . but a vast quantity of produce is collected from the
trees in the gardens of natives, who also compete largely with
the Europeans in the growth of coffee.

Estimate of the Revenue and Expenditure of the Government of Ceylon for the year 1861.

RECEIPTS.

Item	£
Arrears of Reven. of former years	6,500
Customs	200,000
Port and Harbour dues	5,250
Land sales	25,000
Land Revenue	85,000
Rents, exclusive of land	54,000
Licenses	115,000
Stamps	46,000
Taxes	6,500
Postage	1,200
Fines, forfeitures,& fees of Court	5,500
Government vessels	4,000
Sale of Government property	100,002
Ration stoppages from Her Majesty's troops	4,300
Reimbursements in aid of expenses incurred by Government	15,000
Miscellaneous receipts	3,500
Interest	2,000
Pearl Fishery	00
Special receipts	500
Receipts by the Agent General in London	2,000
Total	**681,250**

DISBURSEMENTS.

Item	£	s.	d.	£	s.	d.	£	s.	d.
Charges specially sanctioned by H. M. Government.									
Colonial pay and allowances				39,171	0	7¼			
Contribution towards Military expenditure				24,000	0	0			
Charges sanctioned by Ordinances No. 1 of 1858, & No. 11 of 1859.									
Civil Establishments	52,388	15	4						
Agents of provinces	39,525	18	0						
Judicial Establishments	44,356	0	0						
Ecclesiastical Establishments	9,307	8	0						
Educational Establishments	3,200	16	0						
Medical Establishments	7,657	4	0						
Police Establishments	1,700	0	0						
Fiscals in the provinces	8,796	2	6						
Colonial Commissary	4,090	9	6	171,021	13	4			
Charges voted by the Legislative Council							234,192	13	11¼
							456,268	9	0¼
							690,461	3	0
Deduct probable savings on the above disbursements							10,000	0	0
							680,461	3	0
Surplus Revenue							788	17	0
Total,							**681,250**	**0**	**0**

W. C. GIBSON, *Acting Col. Secretary.*

CHAPTER, VIII.

Conclusion.

In bringing this book to an end, we shall add but a few words. About the year, 1679, an Englishman of the name of Knox, who had for a length of time been a captive in the Kandian country, effected his escape to the sea-coast, and eventually succeeded in returning to England, where he published in a simple, yet truthful manner, a narrative of his adventures, and a description of the land of his captivity. Amongst other things, he drew a picture of the abject condition of the people under the despotism of an unfeeling king, and the oppression of rapacious nobles. The punishments inflicted on those who offended the sovereign, were cruel in the extreme. Mutilation, dismemberment by elephants, and impalement were among those most common. It was a capital offence for a man to whitewash his house, this being a royal prerogative; and none of the humbler classes could venture to manifest the appearance of wealth, lest their so doing should provoke spoliation by the more powerful. If we compare this state of things with the freedom now enjoyed alike by all classes, it must be admitted that the condition of the people has been much improved; and although in the more remote districts of the interior, where knowledge and civilization have yet made but little progress, there may be a yearning after the days gone by, still it may be said, that, as a rule, the people of Ceylon are happy and contented. When in 1857—8, the wave of rebellion swept over the greater part of the continent of India, threatening to carry every thing before it, in its headlong course, not a ripple

disturbed the smooth surface of events in Ceylon, and
the Governor, Sir Henry Ward, had sufficient confidence
in the loyalty of the inhabitants, to enable him to send reinforcements to Bengal, reserving only our faithful
regiment of Riflemen, and a handful of European troops.

At a place called Peredinia, four miles from Kandy,
where a bridge, constructed of satin wood, spans with a
single arch, the broad channel of the Mahawelli ganga,
there is a garden, in which the indigenous productions of Ceylon grow side by side with exotics trans-
ported from distant lands. Both classes of plants
are alike the objects of the superintendent's care, who,
discriminating between the wants of each, seeks the
full development of both. What suits the consti-
tution of the one, would prove fatal to the other;
and in the right discernment of the requirements of each,
lies the difficulty of his task. So is it also, with the
government of a country like Ceylon, inhabited by a
mixed community. To maintain harmony,—to adapt
himself to the peculiar wants of each body,—to secure
the simultaneous development of the whole,—is a task
which would tax the powers of the most able ruler. It is
comparatively easy for a right thinking man of common
sense and energy, to be the autrocrat of a people accustomed implicitly to obey. It is comparatively easy too,
to be the chief magistrate of an enlightened republic. It is
not so easy to hold the reins of government aright,
when a nation is bursting into freedom, and shaking off
the shackles that enthralled it, and in the first impulse
of a new felt power, is disposed to career onwards
too rapidly, and to throw aside restraint of all kind. But
more difficult still is it, to hold the helm, where western

and eastern races are intermingled,—where, instead of freedom being born of the masses, and fostered by the government, it is bestowed on the people by their rulers,—unasked,—and sometimes even uncared for. It is no light task, to steer clearly through the complications arising from the pushing energy of the Saxon, and the conservative tenacity of the Asiatic;—to maintain the rights of those who have staked their all in the land of their adoption, and have brought British thought and feeling with them, and at the same time to consult the interests of the natives, who are equally entitled to the protection of Her Majesty's Government.

If, in forming an estimate of the government of Ceylon, we bear these facts in mind, we shall be justified in saying that the system pursued is judicious, and well adapted to the wants of the country ; and it is our conviction that those entrusted with the framing of the laws, sincerely desire to do what they believe to be best for the welfare of the island.

To conclude.—Let us remind our readers of the important fact, that it is *righteousness* that " exalteth a nation"—that Britain owes her prosperity to her principles ; *and that it is her duty to maintain those principles in all climes, and to exemplify them amongst all classes.* Convinced as the writer is, that the principles of THE BOOK OF GOD are the foundation of moral and of social progress, he lays down his pen with the hope that its truths may be received and adopted by all who dwell in Ceylon, without distinction of race, sex, or degree.

APPENDIX.

Native Sovereigns of Ceylon.

Names, and relationship of each succeeding Sovereign.	Accession.	
1. Wejaya Founder of the Wejayah dynasty,	B. C.	543
2. Oopatissa 1st. Minister—regent, "	"	505
3. Panduwaasa, Paternal nephew of Wejaya;	"	504
4. Abhaya, son of Panduwaasa dethroned,	"	474
Interregnum,	"	454
5. Pandukuabhay, Matern, Grandson of Pandu-waasa,	"	437
6. Mootaseewa, Paternal grandson,	"	367
7. Devenipeatissa, Second son,	"	307
8. Oottiya, fourth son of Mootaseewa,	"	267
9. Maha-seewa. fifth do	"	257
10. Suratissa, sixth do put to death	"	247
11. Sena and Goottika, foreign usurpers—put to death,	"	237
12. Asela, ninth son of Mootaseewa—deposed,	"	215
13. Elaala, foreign usurper—killed in battle,	"	205
14. Dootoogaimoonoo, son of *Kaawantissa*,	"	161
15. Saiduitissai. Brother	"	137
16 Toohl or Thullathanaka, younger son—deposed,	"	119
17. Laiminitissa 1st or Lajjetissa, elder brother,	"	119
18. Kaloonna or Khallaa-a-naaga, brother—put to death,	"	109
19. Walagambahoo 1st or Wattagaamini, brother—deposed,	"	104
20. {Bulahattha, Baayiha, Panaymaaraa, Pelivamaaraa, Daathiya, } 14.7—Foreign usurpers —successively deposed and put to death.	"	103
	"	100
	"	98
	"	91
	"	90
21. Walagambahoo 1st reconquered the kingdom,	"	88
22. Mahaidailitissa or Mahachoola, Son	"	76
23. Choora Naaga, Son—put to death,	"	62
24. Kooda Tissa, Son—poisoned by his wife,	"	50
25. Anoo], widow,	"	47
26. Masantantissa or Kallakanni Tissa, second son of Koodatissa,	"	41
27. Baatiyatissa 1st or Baatikaabhaya, Son,	"	19
28. Maha Dailiya Maana or Daathika, Brother,	A. D.	9
29. Addagaimoono or Aamanda Gaamini, Son—put to death,	"	21

Names, and relationship of each succeeding Sovereign.	Accession.	
30. Kinihirridaila or Kanijaani Tissa, Brother,	A. D.	30
31. Kooda Abhaa or Choolaabhaya, Son,	"	33
32. Singhawalle or Seewalli, Sister—put to death	"	34
Interregnum, - - -	"	35
33. Elloona or Illa Naaga, Maternal nephew of Addagaimoonoo, - - -	"	38
34. Sanda Moohoona or Chanda Mukha Seewa Son, - - - -	"	44
35. Yasa Siloo or Yataalakatissa, Brother—put to death, - - - -	"	52
36. Subha, Usurper—put to death, - -	"	60
37. Wahapp or Wasahba, descendant of Laiminitissa, - - - - -	"	66
38. Waknais or Wanka Naasika, Son, -	"	110
39. Gajaabahoo 1st or Gaaminee, Son, -	"	113
40. Mahaloomaana or Mallaka Naaga, Maternal cousin, - - - ,	"	125
41. Baatiya Tissa 2d or Bhaatika Tissa, Son,	"	131
42. Choola Tissa or Kanitthatissa, Brother,	"	155
43. Koohoona or Choodda Naaga, Son—murdered,	"	173
44. Koodanaama or Kooda Naaga, Nephew—deposed, - - - -	"	183
45. Kooda Sirinaa or Siri Naaga 1st brother-in-law	"	184
46. Waiwahairatissa or Wairatissa, Son-murdered	"	209
47. Abha Sen or Abha Tissa, Brother, -	"	231
48. Siri Naga 2d, Son, - - -	"	239
49. Weja Indoo or Wijaya 2d, Son—put to death,	"	241
50. Sangatissa 1st, descendant of Laiminitissa—poisoned, - - - -	"	242
51. Dahama Sirisanga Bo or Sirisanga Bodhi 1st Do. do.—deposed,	"	246
52. Gooloo Abhaa, Gothaabhaya or Meghawarna Abhaya, Do. do., - -	"	248
53. Makalan Detoo Tissa 1st, Son, -	"	261
54. Maha Sen, Brother, - - -	"	275
55. KitsiriMaiwan 1st or Keertissree Megha warna, Son, - - -	"	302
56. Detoo Tissa 2d, Brother, - -	"	330
57. Bujas or Budha Daasa, Son, - -	"	330
58. Oopatissa 2d, Son, - - -	"	368
59. Maha Naama, Brother, - - -	"	410
60. Senghot or Sotthi Sena, Son—poisoned,	"	432
61. Laimini Tissa 2d, or Chatagaahaka, descendant of Laiminitissa, - -	"	432
62. Mitta Sena or Karalsora, not specified—put to death, - - - -	"	433

Names, and relationship of each succeeding Sovereign.	Accession.
63. { Paandu, Paarinta, Kooda, Khudda Paarinda, Daatthiya, Pitthiya, } 24.9.—Foreign usurpers,	A. D. 434 " 439 " 455 " 455 " 458
64. Daasenkelleya or Dhaatu Sena, descendant of the original royal family—put to death,	" 459
65. Seegiri Kasoomboo or Kaasyapa 1st, Son—committed suicide, -	" 477
66. Moogallaana 1st, Brother, - -	" 495
67. Koomaara Daas or Koomaara Dhaatu Sena, —Son—immolated himself, - -	" 513
68. Kirti Sena, Son—murdered, -	" 522
69. Maidee Seewoo or Seewaka, maternal uncle —murdered, - -	" 531
70. Laimini Oopatissa 3d, brother-in-law, -	" 531
71. Ambaherra Salamaiwan or Siluakaala, son-in-law, - - -	" 534
72. Daapuloo 1st or Daatthaapa Bhodhi, second son—committed suicide, -	" 547
73. Dalamagalan or Moogallaana 2d, elder brother	" 547
74. Kuda Kitsiri Maiwan 1st or Keertisree Meghawarna, Son—put to death, -	" 567
75. Senewee or Maha Naaga, descendant of the Okaaka branch, - -	" 586
76. Aggrabodhi 1st or Akbo, maternal nephew,	" 589
77. Aggrabodhi 2d or Soola Akbo, son-in-law,	" 623
78. Sanghatissa, Brother—decapitated, -	" 633
79. Boona Moogalan or Laimini Bonaaya, usurper—put to death, - -	" 633
80. Abhaseggaaheka or Asiggaaheka, maternal grandson, - - -	" 639
81. Siri Sangabo 2d, Son—deposed, -	" 645
82. Kaloona Detootissa or Laimina Katooreya, descendant of Laiminitissa—committed suicide, - - -	" 645
Siri Sangabo 2d, restored, and again deposed,	" 649
83 Daloopintissa 1st or Dhattbopatissa Laimini branch—killed in battle, - -	" 665
84. Paisooloo Kasoombo or Kaasypa 2d, brother of Sirisangabo, - - -	" 677
85. Dapuloo 2d, Okaaka branch—deposed,	" 686
86. Daloopeatissa 2d or Kattha-Datthopatissa, son of Daloopeatissa 1st, -	" 693
87. Paisooloo Siri Sanga Bo 3d, or Aggrabodhi, Brother - - - -	" 702

Names, and relationship of each succeeding Sovereign.	*Accession.*
88. Walpitti Wasidata or Dantanaama, Okaaka branch,	A. D.
	" 718
89. Hoonoonaru Riandala or Hatthadatha, original royal family—decapitated,	" 720
90. Mahalaipaanoo or Maanawamma, do. do. do.	" 720
91. Kaasiyappa 3d or Kasoombo, Son,	" 726
92. Aggrabodhi 3d or Akbo, Nephew,	" 729
93. Aggrabodhi 4th or Kuda Akbo, Son,	" 769
94. Mihindoo 1st or Salamaiwan, original royal family,	" 775
95. Dappoola 2d, Son,	" 795
96. Mihindoo 2d or Dharmika-Seelaamaiga, Son,	" 800
97. Aggrabodhi 5th or Akbo, Brother,	" 804
98. Dappoola 3d or Kuda Duppoola, Son,	" 815
99. Aggrabodhi 6th cousin,	" 831
100. Mitwella Sen or Selaamaiga, Son,	" 838
101. Kaasiyappa 4th or Maaganyin Sena or Mihindoo, Grandson,	" 858
102. Udaya 1st Brother,	" 891
103. Udaya 2d, Son,	" 926
104. Kaasiyappa 5th nephew and son-in-law,	" 937
105. Kaasiyappa 6th, son-in-law,	" 954
106. Dappoola 4th, Son,	" 964
107. Dappoola 5th, not specified,	" 964
108. Udaya, 3d, Brother,	" 974
109. Sena 2d, not specified.	" 977
110. Udaya 4th, do do.	" 986
111. Sena 3d, do. do.	" 991
112. Mihindoo 3d, do. do	" 997
113. Sena 4th, Son—minor,	" 1013
114. Mihindoo 4th, Brother—carried captive to India—during the Soleean conquest,	" 1023
Interregnum Soleean vice-royalty,	" 1059
115. Wejayabahoo 1st or Sirisangabo 4th Grandson of Mihindoo 4th,	" 1071
116. Jayabahoo 1st, Brother,	" 1126
117. Wikramabahoo 1st ⎫ Manaabarana ⎪ 118. Gajnabahoo 2d, ⎬ A disputed succession. Siriwallaba or Kusiri Maiwan ⎭	" 1127
119. Prakramabaho 1st, son of Maanaabarana,	" 1153
120. Wijayabahoo 2d, nephew—murdered,	" 1186
121 Mihindo 5th or Kitsen Kisdaas, usurper—put to death,	" 1187
122. Kirti Nissanga, a prince of Kaalinga,	" 1187
Weerabahoo, son—put to death,	" 1196

14

Names, and relationship of each succeeding Sovereign.	Accession.
123. Wikramabahoo 2d, brother of Kirti Nissanga—put to death, - - -	A. D. " 1196
124. Chondakanga, nephew—deposed, -	" 1196
125. Leelawatee, widow of Prakramabahoo—deposed, - - -	" 1197
126. Saahasamallawa, Okaaka branch—deposed,	" 1200
127. Kalyaanawati, sister of Kirti Nissanga, -	" 1202
128. Dharmaasooka, not specified—a minor,	" 1208
129. Nayaanga or Neekanga, minister, put to death	" 1209
Leelawatee, restored, and again deposed,	" 1209
130. Lokaiswera 1st, usurper—deposed, -	" 1210
Leelawatee, again restored and deposed a third time, - - - -	" 1211
131. Pandi Prakramabahoo 2d, usurper—deposed,	" 1211
132. Maagha, foreign usurper, - [1st,	" 1214
133. Wejayabahoo 3d, descendant of Sirisangabo,	" 1235
134. Kalik. ala Sahitya Sargwajnya or Paandita Prakramabahoo 3d, Son, - -	" 1266
135. Bosat Wejayabahoo 4th, Son, - -	" 1301
136. Bhuwanekabahoo 1st, Brother, - [1st,	" 1303
137. Prakramabahoo 3d, son of Bosat Wejayabaho,	" 1314
138. Bhuwanekabahoo 2d, son of Bhuwanekabaho	" 1319
139. Pandita Prakramabahoo 4th, not specified,	
140. Wanny Bhuwanekabahoo 3d, do.	
141. Wejayabahoo 5th, do.	
142. Bhuwanekabahoo 4th, do.	" 1347
143. Prakramabahoo 5th, do.	" 1361
144. Wikramabahoo 3d, cousin, do.	" 1371
145. Bhuwanekabahoo 5th, not specified, -	" 1378
146. Wejayabahoo 5th, or Weerabahoo, do.	" 1398
147. Sree Prakramabahoo 6th, do.	" 1410
148. Jayaabahoo 2d, maternal grandson—put to death, - - - -	" 1462
149. Bhuwanekabahoo 6th, not specified,	" 1464
150. Pundita Prakramabahoo 7th, adopted son,	" 1471
151. Weera Prakramabahoo 8th brother of Bhuwanekabahoo 6th, - - -	" 1485
152. Dharma Prakramabahoo 9th, Son, -	" 1505
153. Wejayabahoo 7th Brother—murdered, -	" 1527
154. Bhuwanekabahoo 7th, Son, - -	" 1534
155. Don Juan Dharmapaala, - -	" 1542
156. Raajasingha 1st, son of *Maayaadunnai*,	" 1581
157. Wimala Dharma, original royal family,	" 1592
158. Senaaratena or Senerat, Brother, -	" 1604
159. Raajasingha 2d, Son, - - -	" 1635
160. Wimala Dharma Suriya 2d, son of Rajasinga,	" 1685
161. Sreeweera Prakrama Narendrasingha or Koondasaala, Son, - -	" 1707

Names, and relationship of each succeeding Sovereign.	Accession.
162. Sreewejaya Raajasingha or Hanguranketta, brother-in-law, - - - -	A. D. " 1730
163. Kirtisree Rajasingha, brother-in law, -	" 1747
164. Raajaadhi Raajasingha, Brother, -	" 1781
165. Sree Wickrema Raajasingha, son of the late king's wife's sister, deposed by the English and died in captivity, - -	" 1798

Captains General and Governors of Ceylon.

Whilst in possession of the Portuguese.

Pedro Lopez de Souza,
Jerome de Azevedo,
Francois de Menezes,
Manuel Mascarenhas Homen,
Nanha Alvares Pereira,
Constantin de Say Noranha,
George d'Albuque,
Constantin de Say Noranha,
D. George d'Almeida,
Diego de Melho,
Antoine Mascarenhas,

Phillippe Mascarenhas,
Manuel Mascarenhas Homen,
Francois de Mello Castro,
Antoine de Souza Continho,
under whose administration Colombo was surrendered to the Dutch,
A. D. Merely Menezes *last Captain General in command of Jaffna and Manaar.*

Governors of Ceylon.

WITH THE DATES WHEN THEIR ADMINISTRATION COMMENCED.

Whilst in possession of the Dutch.

Willem Jacobezen Coster, Commander at the surrender of Galle, - - -	13th March 1640.
Jan Thuysz, President and Governor at Galle, - - - - -	21st Aug. 1640.
Joau Matsoyker, Ordinary Councillor and Governor at Galle, - - - -	24th May 1640.
Jacob Van Kittenstein Governor at Galle,	25th Feb. 1650.
Adrian Van Der Meyden, Governor at Galle	11th Oct. 1653.
Adrian Van Der Meyden, Governor at Colombo, - - - - - -	12th May 1656.
Ryklof Van Goens, Governor—Administration commenced, - - - -	12th May 1663.
Jacob Hustar, Extraordinary Councillor of India, and Governor, - - -	27th Dec. 1663.
Ryklof Van Goens, administered the Government from, - - - -	19th Nov. 1664.
Lourens Van Peil, Commander, President Governor, and Extraordinary Councillor of India, - - - - - -	3d. Dec. 1680.

Thomas Van Rhee, Governor and Extraordinary Councillor of India, - -	10th Jan.	1693.
Paulus de Rhoo, appointed Governor and Director of Ceylon, - - -	29th Jan.	1695.
Gerrit De Heer, Governor, - -	22d Feb.	1697.
The Members of Council, - -	26th Nov.	1702.
Mr. Cornelis Johannes Simonsz Governor.	11th May	1703.
Hendrick Becker, Governor and Extraordinary Councillor, - - -	22d Dec.	1707.
Mr. Isaack Augustin Rumph, Governor and Extraordinary Councillor of India, -	7th Dec.	1716.
Arnold Moll, Commander at Galle, -	11th June	1723.
Johannes Hertenberg, Governor, -	12th Jan.	1724.
Jan Paulus Schagen, Commander at Galle.	19th Oct.	1725.
Petrus Vuyst, Governor and Extraordinary Councillor of India, - - -	16th Sept.	1726.
Stephanus Versluys, Governor and Extraordinary Councillor of India, [pattam,	27th Aug.	1729.
Gualterus Woutersz, Commander of Jaffna-	25th Aug.	1732.
Jacob Christian Pielaat, Extraordinary Councillor of India and Commissary, -	21st Dec.	1732.
Dederic Van Donburg, Governor, -	21st Jan.	1734.
Jan Maccara, Commander of Galle, -	7th June	1736.
Gustaff Willem Baaron Van Inhoff, Extraordinary Councillor of India and Governor,	23d July	1736.
Willem Maurits Bruininck Governor,	12th March	1740.
Daniel Overbeek Governor and Extraordinary Councillor of India, - -	3d Jan.	1742.
Julius Valentyn Stein Van Gollnesse, Extraordinary Councillor of India and Governor,	11th May	1743.
Gerard Van Vreeland, Extraordinary Councillor of India and Governor, - -	6th March	1751.
Jacob De Jong, Commander of Jaffnapattam,	26th Feb.	1751.
Joan Gideon Loten, Extraordinary Councillor of I dia and Governor, - -	30th Sept.	1752.
Jan Schreuder, Extraordinary Councillor of India and Governor, - -	17th March	1757.
Lubbert Jan Baron Van Eck, Governor under whose administration Kandy was taken on the 9th February, 1763, - - [pattam,	11th Nov.	1762.
Anthony Mooyaart, Commander of Jaffna-	13th May	1765.
Iman Willem Falck, Governor and Director of India,	9th August	1765.
Willem Jacob Van De Graaf, Extraordinary Councillor of India and Governor, -	7th Feb.	1785.
Joan Gerard Van Angelbeek, Ordinary Councillor of India and Governor, under whose administration Colombo surrendered to the arms of His Britannic Majesty on the, -	16th Feb.	1796

English Governors.

The Honorable the Governor of Madras in Council, - - - - - -	16th Feb.	1796.
Hon. Frederick North, (late Earl of Guildford,) - - - - - - -	12th Oct.	1798.
Lieutenant General Right Hon. Sir Thomas Maitland, G. C. B., - - - -	19th July	1805.
Major General John Wilson, Lieutenant Governor, - - - - -	19th March	1811.
General Sir R. Brownrigg, Bart. G. C. B.,	11th March	1812.
Major General Sir Edward Barnes, K. C. B., Lieutenant Governor, - - -	1st Feb.	1820.
Lieut. Gen. The Hon. Sir E. Paget, K. C. B.	2d Feb.	1822.
Major Gen. Sir James Campbell, K. C. B., Lieutenant Governor, - - -	6th Nov.	1822.
Lieut. Gen. Sir Edward Barnes, K. C. B.,	18th Jan.	1824.
Major General Sir John Wilson, K. C. B., Lieutenant Governor, - - -	13th Oct.	1831.
The Right Hon. Sir Robert Wilmot Horton Bart. G. C. H., - - - - -	23d Oct.	1831.
The Right Hon. James Alexander Stewart Mackenzie, - - - - -	7th Nov.	1837.
Lieut. Gen. Sir Colin Campbell, K. C. B.,	5th April	1841.
Sir J. E. Tennent, K. C. S. Lieut. Governor,	19th April	1847.
The Right Hon. the Viscount Torrington,	29th May	1847.
The Hon. C. J. MacCarthy, Esq. Lieutenant Governor, - - -	18th Oct.	1850.
Sir Geo. W. Anderson, K. C. B., -	27th Nov.	1850.
The Hon. C. J. MacCarthy, Esq. Lieutenant Governor, - - -	18th Jan.	1855.
Sir Henry George Ward, K. G. C. M. G ,	11th May	1855.
Major General Henry Frederic Lockyer, C. B., K. H., Lieutenant Governor, -	30th June	1860.
Colonel Charles Edmund Wilkinson, R. E. Lieutenant Governor, - - -	30th July	1860.
Sir Charles Justin MacCarthy, Kt. -	22d Oct.	1860.

ETURN OF THE POPULATION, &c. IN 1859, FROM THE ALMANAC, of 1861.

ES.	Area in Square Miles.	WHITES.		COLOURED POPULATION.		TOTAL.		Aliens and resident strangers not included in preceding columns.	Population to the square mile.	Persons employed in		
		Males.	Females.	Males.	Fem.	Males.	Fem.			Agriculture.	Manufacture.	Commerce.
· · ·	3,820	1,398	1,344	302,707	272,779	304,105	274,123	9,109	153.75	164,561	19,656	34,647
· · ·	3,362	114	82	107,489	101,138	107,603	101,220	5,672	63.79	124,931	3,310	7,629
· · ·	2,147	238	262	162,788	153,520	163,026	153,782	1,972	148.47	86,505	16,634	27,088
· · ·	4,753	136	148	40,017	36,756	40,153	36,904	387	16.29	19,447	1,200	2,652
· · ·	5,427	363	355	155,703	151,489	156,066	151,844	564	56.84	172,275	4,205	4,975
· · ·	5,191	616	278	142,401	121,469	143,017	121,747	14,744	53.84		5,526	14,169
sive of ry)	24,700	2,865	2,469	911,105	837,151	913,970	839,620	32,448	72.30	567,719	50,533	91,160
il Ord- with ies.												
· · ·	3,820	950	125	921	541	1,871	666	"	.66	"	"	"
· · ·	3,362	1	1	35	31	36	32	"	.02	"	"	"
· · ·	2,147	100	22	375	222	475	244	"	.33	"	"	"
· · ·	4,753	179	19	327	209	506	228	"	.15	"	"	"
· · ·	5,427	2	2	81	64	83	66	"	.02	"	"	"
· · ·	5,191	212	38	460	317	672	355	"	.19	"	"	"
ry	24,700	1,444	207	2,199	1,384	3,643	1,591	"	.21	"	"	"
l ·	24,700	4,309	2,676	913,304	838,535	917,613	841,211	32,448	72.52	567,719	50,533	91,160

CORRECTIONS.

PAGE. 3. We have been informed on the best
" ' authority, that the Mahawelle ganga
" ' takes its rise in Pethuru Tallegalle.
" 4. In Colombo, the thermometer some-
" ' times rises so high as 90° 3′ 0″, in
" ' April, and falls so low as 68° 4′ 0″, in
" ' January.
" 14. Kurnegalle, lies north *west* of Kandy.
" " The highest offices of a *local* character,
" " are those of Maniagar and Odiar; but the
" " Modeliars of the Courts and Cutcheries,
" " would doubtless have the precedence.
" 39. For *three* parts, read *four* parts.

www.ingramcontent.com/pod-product-compliance
Lightning Source LLC
Chambersburg PA
CBHW031114020726
47495CB00007B/2199